ARMOR'S MISTAKE

SATAN'S RAIDERS MC
BOOK THREE

ELIZABETH KNOX

Armor's Mistake

This book is a work of fiction. The names, characters, places, and incidents are all products of the author's imagination and are not to be construed as real. Any resemblances to persons, organizations, events, or locales are entirely coincidental.

Armor's Mistake. Copyright © 2022 by Elizabeth Knox. All rights reserved. No part of this book may be used or reproduced in any manner whatsoever without written permission from the author, except in the case of brief quotations used in articles or reviews. For information, contact E. Knox.

Editing: Kim Lubbers, Knox Publishing

Proofreading: Marybeth Higgins, Knox Publishing

Formatting: R. Epperson, Knox Publishing

Cover Designer: Clarise Tan, CT Cover Creations

Photographer: Wander Aguiar

❀ Created with Vellum

SATAN'S RAIDERS MC MEMBERS:

Breaker — Prez
Chains — VP
Ops — Enforcer
p. Mabel
Armor — Road Captain
Killer — Sgt. at Arms
Sarge — Full Patch
Brick — Full Patch
Ice — Full Patch
p. Sunny
Children: Octavia
Inc (in Montana)— Full Patch
p. Octavia & Zane
Children: Neo, 1 year 8 months (Inc)
Agony — Full Patch
Fury — Full Patch
Archer — Prospect

PROLOGUE

Armor

Five Months Ago . . .

"Man, if I get in trouble because of your ass, I might just beat the livin' shit outta you. Your club doesn't know a thing about this, but Inc does?" Hammer chastises me as he sits in the passenger seat of my truck.

The club doesn't know about this because it isn't their business. "This is personal, man. I told you that. The club doesn't need to know about it because it's my business."

Hammer leans back in his seat and raises both of his brows as I drive. "The club knows about everyone's business, brother. Doesn't matter if it's personal or not. You know as well as I do that when we're in a club, they're our family, and our families are notorious for not keeping their noses in their shit. They're too busy focusing on everyone else's." Hammer isn't wrong, but I understand Zane runs things a bit differently up in Montana.

Hammer here isn't part of the Satan's Raiders MC. He's part of the Reapers Rejects MC, but since the Reapers Rejects has Inc as their regent, we have Hammer as ours. The goal with regency is to offer a bit of security in our alliance, but it's also collateral. If one person was to betray us from the Reapers Rejects, we'd have an instant hostage, plus Hammer's family if it came to that. Now, I don't think it ever would, considering my president's sister is married to the president of the Reapers Rejects MC.

"We're not like that. Everyone has secrets. I can guarantee it. We know about some but not about others. For example, it was a huge secret Inc had been with Zane and Octavia after they were married, and even though their secret saw the light of day, it was still a secret for some time. My point is, everyone has something they're hiding. Every single one of us," I tell Hammer, hoping he'll see why I'm so particular about not telling the club. The truth is, Inc was one of the few people who knew about what I do on the side, and when Inc left Los Angeles, it left me doing this by myself. Now, I have a pretty good reputation with my contacts, but that doesn't mean something might not go wrong. It's always better to operate on the side of caution, which is why Inc pulled Hammer in on this. He didn't want me to go out and continue to do this by myself. I was irritated at first because he didn't even ask me about it, but Inc is a true friend. One who gives a damn about my well-being.

"Yep, and I'm here tellin' you that one way or another, this little thing you got goin' on is gonna see that light of day, just like everythin' else. People can't keep secrets for long, brother. It always comes out, and I hope for your sake Breaker doesn't condemn you for it. You're all in enough hot water right now as it is." We're only in hot water because there's a fucking rat amongst our ranks or close to us. Once we find out who it is, our club won't be so torn apart. But until then, I have to keep helping these kids. I can't just let them get sold to people who want to turn them into sex slaves or traffic them to other countries. Most of the kids being sold aren't even American ones. Fuck, these bastards have packages called 'all you can eat', which means you get one child from every country they've pulled from that week. It's disgusting and downright immoral.

"When it does, I'll deal with the consequences. Now, the bus is in downtown LA right now, yeah?"

Hammer nods beside me as he picks up his phone. "It should be here within the hour. We'll get your deal solidified, and then we'll get them on the bus." I made a deal with Zane, with Inc's help, to get these kids up to Billings. Montana is a decent place, to begin with, but all I've ever wanted is to make sure these kids are going to a safe place. The Reapers Rejects have their reputation when it comes to taking in people who need a safe place to rest their heads. They're saints in my book, especially for helping me get these kids off the streets and out of devious people's hands.

My deal with Zane is that I pay for the kids, get them sent up to Montana, and he makes sure they have a roof over their heads and anything they might need. Eventually, if it's safe to reunite them with their parents or even next of kin, he will. In some cases, it isn't safe for the children to go back to where they came from. In those cases, the Reapers Rejects work with some of their contacts, usually mafia affiliates who have politicians and government workers in their pockets, to get birth certificates for the children. This way, they're always safe with the Reapers Rejects.

"Good. We need everything ready for them," I comment.

This is Hammer's first time assisting me with purchasing the children, and I'm certain he's going to learn a lot more about what I do and why I do it when he sees these children.

"Yeah, everything's good, man. Now, I gotta ask you somethin'."

I glance over at Hammer for a split second before averting my gaze back to the road. "Shoot."

"How is it you do this? I mean, you have to pay for them somehow. It's not like these people let you walk away with these kids."

He's right. I don't just walk away without giving them something. "I might not look like it, given the tattoos and the rugged look, but I'm a trust fund baby. I have millions and millions of dollars I'll never use. Honestly, I think it's all bullshit. My father made money from good ol' American capitalism, as did his father and his father before him. This money I have is made from the sweat, blood, and tears of hardworking American people . . . and I want to do something good with it. So, I've made it my mission to bring down people who orchestrate things such as this. I'm slowly getting closer to developing a good relationship with the man I buy from, and after my orders increase over time, I'll have a reputation. That's what I want. I want a way to get closer to the top, closer to the head of this beast, so I can personally remove it from its body."

"Shit, you're a dark son of a bitch. Now I know why Inc was good friends with you." I laugh at Hammer's comment, and the GPS informs me my turn is coming up, so I pay attention to the map and follow the rest of the directions.

Otis is my contact, and we never meet in the same place. The first couple of times, we did, but after that, we didn't. My guess is he was suspicious I might've been an undercover cop, so he was testing me.

I pull into the abandoned parking lot, and sure enough, I spot another car in the lot. The sun's just set, and I flash my lights twice at the other car, which then flashes its lights at me in return. We both shut off our vehicles, and Hammer gets out of his side while I get out on mine. I walk toward the middle, and Otis looks at Hammer and then at me.

"Otis, it's good to see you again. This is my business associate, Calvin. I hope you don't mind I've brought him here. He's looking to see if he can get in on this as a partner with me. It means my orders will be increasing, so I hope that won't be a problem."

Otis' eyes nearly pop out of his head. "Problem? No, sir. No problem at all. What're you looking for right now?"

"Depends on what you have in stock," I comment and pull a cigarette out of my pocket. I wait for Otis to speak and light it, and just as I'm taking my first inhale, he finally speaks up.

"I got a little bit of everything. Chinese, Czech, Russian, what suits your fancy?"

I look at Hammer for a minute and then look back over to Otis. "Gimme ten Russians, ten Chinese, and five Czech." From the way Otis' expression is shifting, I can tell he likes what I'm saying.

"All right. When do you want to pick them up?"

"I have transportation here tonight, so tonight."

"Certainly. I can do that. Can you give me two hours to get everything ready and verify the payment?"

"You won't need time to verify the payment, Otis. Just tell me how much it is for all of them, and I'm hoping you're gonna give me some sort of discount since I'm taking twenty-five mouths to feed off your hands."

"Yeah, yeah. Mmm, I'll cut you a deal this time. For the lot of them, throw me a hundred and fifty." I nod at what he's saying. I figured I'd be paying at least two hundred for all of them, so I walked back to my truck and left Hammer with Otis. I brought two duffel bags, so I grabbed fifteen ten-thousand straps of hundred-dollar bills and threw them in the empty bag, zipped it up, and headed back over to the two men. I hand it to Otis, and he opens the bag, surely counting the straps. "I'll get them ready for you. Can your transport come here? I'll have my people get everything ready."

"Yeah, that won't be a problem. I'll have them meet you

back here in two hours to get the shipment," I tell Otis, and we shake hands. "Next time, it'll be more, as long as my partner here likes what we get this time."

Otis looks over to Hammer. "Calvin, I assure you the people I work with are only seeking the highest quality. I'm sure you'll be satisfied."

"We'll see about that," Hammer comments before he walks back to the truck. His words leave Otis worried about the next shipment, and I'm glad. It'll make him sweat a little bit, and if I'm lucky, he'll talk about one of his buyers upping his funds.

One way or another, I'm going to make my way to the top.

CHAPTER ONE

JADA

Present Day . . .

I had this planned out great, or at least I thought it was planned out great. I was going to surprise my brother, who I hadn't seen in quite some time, and he'd be overjoyed at my visit. At least, I thought he would. Little did I know that there was a big event going on in Los Angeles right now and that there wouldn't be any taxis, Uber drivers, or Lyft drivers around. I had it planned that I would show up at the Satan's Raiders MC's bar, *The Clubhouse*, and Hammer would see me. I figured he'd be excited since he left Billings to be down here almost five months ago.

Since our parents passed away, it's been really hard for me to be in Billings by myself. I know I'm not really alone, considering the Reapers Rejects MC has always made me feel like I'm part of their family too, but it isn't the same as having my brother around. Hammer and I went through the good and the bad together for our entire lives. When he told me he had to move to Los Angeles for the club, I was taken aback by what he said. Part of me thinks he didn't just move because the club wanted him to. Deep down, I think he wanted to move so Shiloh could have a fresh start.

She used to be a club whore with the Reapers Rejects MC, which is a woman who stays with a biker club and does what they want. What they do is exactly in their name, 'whore'. I don't ever want to call Shiloh that, but she slept with a lot of the people in the club, and it's obvious. Maybe that's why Hammer moved, too, because he wanted to be in a place where not everyone fucked Shiloh.

Don't get me wrong, I really like the girl. I think she's great and she's great for my brother. I've never seen him so happy before, and I don't think Shiloh's the type of woman who would ever break his heart.

In a way, I'm a bit envious of the relationship they have. Hammer's found his person, and I'm here, alone. I've dated in the past, but I haven't dated anyone I thought was special. Okay, maybe that's a lie. I dated a guy in high school named Trenton, and he was on the football team. He was okay. He was a sweet boy, and I never thought we'd graduate and then continue our relationship. He had big dreams, and I didn't want any sort of long-term commitment at the time.

I'm on the outside of the airport, leaning against a concrete wall. On the other side of the concrete wall is a garden with various types of flowers. A few people who departed from the same flight as I did are sitting around the wall, waiting for their rides, I'm assuming.

Since I couldn't get another ride to the Satan's Raiders MC clubhouse, I had no choice but to call my brother and let him know what I did. He wasn't exactly too happy about it, probably because it was early. Earlier than he'd like to be awake, I'm going to guess.

Hammer told me he'd be at the airport in about twenty minutes, and it's about that time right now.

"Are you here for business or pleasure? I couldn't help but

stare at you on the plane. Your beauty is something rare these days," a man's deep voice comes up from beside me.

I look him up and down. He might be in his early forties, and he has a five o'clock shadow that's a few days overgrown. Overall, he's a very handsome man with light green eyes and an olive complexion, but he's giving me some serious creeper vibes.

"I don't see how it's any of your business, sir," I tell him and glance down at my phone to look at the time. It's five past nine, and Hammer should be here any moment.

"My name's Ben, not sir. And you, my lovely lady, are?"

"Annoyed because you can't take a hint. I have no interest in having a pointless conversation with you, and I'm not in the mood for your flirtatious remarks. If you want to get fucked, go on Tinder."

Just as I finish speaking, I spot my brother's truck coming up the lane. I wave him down, and he pulls up to the sidewalk. I grab onto my luggage, and at the same time, Ben puts his hand over mine. Naturally bothered, I raise both of my eyebrows. "What the hell are you doing?" I question him with saltiness in my tone.

"I'm helping you unless you'd like to do it yourself," he tells me, and I'm growing more impatient by the moment.

Hammer puts his hazards on and gets out of the truck. "There a problem here or somethin'?" my brother asks. His voice sounds like it's vibrating from his entire body.

"This your husband?" Ben asks.

"I'm her brother, and it doesn't look like she wants you near her right now, my man. I'd suggest you back the fuck up before I make you," Hammer tells him, and Ben cackles.

"I should've known," Ben says, shaking his head.

"Should've known what exactly?" I ask him, crossing my arms in pure frustration and annoyance.

"That you'd be mixed up with some ghetto ass people."

Just as Ben finishes what he's saying, I rear my arm back, ball my hand into a fist and punch upward against his nose. The moment I come into contact with him, his nose cracks, and he stumbles backward. His hands shoot up to his nose, and blood comes oozing out.

Hammer snickers and grabs my luggage, putting it in the back of his truck. "Come on. I think the lesson you just gave him in manners will be one he won't forget."

I do as my brother says and get in the truck, and he gets behind the wheel. He turns his hazards off, and then we take off. I hope my brother's right. I hope Ben won't be such a total ass to other people because saying that sort of shit to the wrong person could get him killed.

"So, why didn't you tell me you were coming into town?" Hammer asks as we pull out of the airport and onto the main road.

"I wanted it to be a surprise. I haven't seen you in a few months, and it really messed with me a bit. I miss you, Hammer. Being home . . . well, it isn't the same without you there."

Hammer nods, and I think it's in agreement. "Are you off work right now? I mean, you took some vacation time to come down here, right?"

I shake my head. "Actually, I didn't. I quit my old job, and I'm doing something where I can travel as little or as much as I want. So, I don't know if you remember, but I told you I was making a YouTube a while back."

Hammer nods a couple of times like he's trying to remember what I'm talking about. "Is that the thing you were doing after hours?"

"Yeah, it's what I was doing on the side while I gained some momentum until I could leave the job I had. You know I never have all of my hands in one bucket, and this was the career move I wanted to make for a really long time."

"Okay, so, uh, what is it?"

"I'm a content creator."

"A content what?" Hammer laughs, and I'm used to this sort of reaction. He thinks it's all fun and games and that it isn't serious at all.

"A content creator. So, I have YouTube, Facebook, TikTok, and all of that. My job is to create content, so for example, every Tuesday, I post a video about tacos, reviewing the best places to get them, history about tacos, etcetera. It kind of goes on and on. I typically post a lot about food, food blogs, and reviews about places to eat. I go to places that have a lot of raves about them, for their crazy cool milkshakes and burgers, etc. It could really be anything."

"And you get paid for this?" Hammer asks me skeptically.

"Yeah, I got my first paycheck last month, and it doubled what I was making at the other place."

"Shit, that's awesome, Jada," Hammer tells me, and I feel pride swell in my chest. It was a big deal to make this career move, and I really do feel like it's finally paying off. "So, why did you have to surprise me? You know I hate that shit more than anything else."

I do know he hates it, but I thought he would've liked me coming down here. "I thought we needed to see each other, especially since mom passed. It was just . . . so fucking hard. We lost dad, and then not even a month later, she passed too. I swear it was a broken heart. She was healthy otherwise, but I think living without a dad was so hard on her."

"I think you're right." My brother has never uttered these words to me before. To say I'm shocked would be an understatement, but I'm glad he agrees with me. "Um, you got a place to stay, like a hotel or somethin'?" Hammer asks, quickly changing the subject.

I shake my head. "Yeah, I'm gonna stay at a Motel 8 outside of Los Angeles. The Yelp reviews looked decent."

"Nu-uh. I ain't gonna have you stayin' at a damn Motel 8. They're sketchy as fuck. You're gonna stay at the club. Even if I have to throw a prospect on the couch, I'm gonna do that."

"Hammer, it's no big deal. I can stay at—" With one stern look from my brother, I stop speaking.

"I said what I said, and I'm not gonna change my mind, Jada." My brother is just as stubborn as our father was, if not more.

It takes us about thirty minutes, but we both arrive at Satan's Raiders MC clubhouse. Hammer drives down the alley around the back and parks the truck, then grabs my luggage, and the two of us walk in through the back. We head downstairs, where the main area is, and we sit and chat for a bit. After a while, Hammer takes me upstairs to where the rooms are for the club members and takes me to what he says is a guest room, but as we approach, the sound of something being cut rings out, and the doors open.

"Uh, that's where I'm supposed to be staying?" I question him, and Hammer puts up his hand while he goes to check it out.

"My man, Sarge, what's goin' on in here?" Hammer asks someone inside the bedroom.

"I'm redoing the flooring and the bathroom. Breaker's been on me about it for a while now. Why? What's up?" the man answers him back.

"My sister is in town, and I thought she could stay here in the guest room."

"Shit, brother. I'm sorry, this won't be ready for another week at least," Sarge tells him, and a man walks by with a cut on. It reads 'Agony'.

"You're gonna have to sleep on the couch for a bit, man. My sister is in town and needs a place to rest her head," my brother tells him, and just as he's speaking to Agony, footsteps are coming up the stairwell.

"Dude, I don't take orders from you, so I don't have to do shit," Agony sassily tells my brother.

"You might not take orders from Hammer, but you know the pecking order with me. Clean your room up and make sure it's presentable for this lovely lady, and make it quick," a man's deep voice comes from behind me, and with every word he speaks, there's an authoritative tone behind it all.

I swallow hard and turn to face the man who's just given me a place to stay, and I'm taken aback a bit. "Um, thank you so much. I'm Jada, by the way."

"I'm Armor. It's lovely to meet you, Jada, and I apologize for Agony's shitty attitude. You won't hear another peep out of him."

I'm sure I won't. The man standing in front of me looks like he would kill people for fun, and I doubt anyone would want to piss him off.

CHAPTER TWO

ARMOR

It's been a week since I met Hammer's vixen of a sister, Jada. Whenever she's around, I can't seem to keep my eyes off her. She's got beautiful, luscious curls that frame her face, and her body is something I'd gladly die for. It's like an hourglass sort of shape, but her hips are thick, and so are her thighs. I'd love to grab hold of them a few times, but I doubt I'd be able to stop once I get started.

Ice is off with Sunny because she's due in the next couple of weeks. They thought she was having contractions this morning, but it turns out they're Braxton Hicks, which is some sort of fake contraction or labor, I guess. I don't know, but I'm sure one day I'm going to learn a lot more about it when I have kids.

Shit, I haven't given that much thought in a while. It seems like a lot of my brothers in the club are starting to settle down. Ice has Sunny, who was an old flame of his. Inc has Octavia and Zane and Ops as Amabel, who we call Mabel. I don't know if love is in the air or what, but all I've ever wanted in life is to be in the club and have a woman by my side no matter what. Only finding a woman like that isn't exactly easy these days. So many of them just want sex with no-strings-attached. I don't blame women like that, but where are the ones who want to wake up by your side every day? Where are the women who want to have a family with you and be with you through thick and thin? That's the type of woman I'm looking for.

I throw my cut over my shoulders and exit my bedroom, shutting the door firmly behind me. I walk down the hallway and descend the stairwell, heading for the bar. It's about two in the afternoon now, and I've already had a busy day. I met up with Otis late last night and purchased another batch of kids. I bought five more than the last time, and they've already been transported up to Billings for the Reapers Rejects MC to help me with. Thank goodness they're on board with this. Otherwise, I wouldn't know what to do with the kids. I always knew I needed to get them out of the circumstances they were in, but I never knew how I was going to do it until I spoke to Inc, and then, in turn, Inc spoke to the Reapers Rejects, and they voted on assisting me with this.

I walk into the bar area of *The Clubhouse*, and Jada's sitting at the end of the bar, speaking to Fury. Her hair's pulled onto the top of her head in a tight bun, and not a single hair's out of place. She's wearing light-wash denim jeans with a black tank top and an army jacket over it, and she's got on some black leather boots. One thing I've noticed about Jada is how she pays attention to her appearance, and I think that's hot as fuck. The woman takes pride in how she looks, and I sure as fuck take notice every time I lay my eyes on her.

Jada's the type of woman who doesn't have to put too much effort into her make-up because her beauty is so natural already. I think she might put a bit of mascara on her eyes and maybe some sort of lip gloss, but other than that, I don't notice anything.

"You know, if my brother's bed is too uncomfortable for you, you could always stay in mine," Fury tells Jada, and I have a hard time biting my tongue as I approach the two of them. I take a seat next to her and cock a brow at him.

"His bed is perfectly fine, but thank you," Jada says, swirling her plastic straw around in what I can assume is Sprite.

"I mean it. Any time you want to come into my bed, you go right ahead. It's an open invitation," Fury continues, and I clear my throat.

"Fury, I'm thinkin' your bike needs to be cleaned." As I speak, Fury meets his eyes with my own. He narrows them after a second and cracks a smile.

"No, it doesn't. Just cleaned it yesterday."

"You never know. Someone might've gone and taken a piss on it. Best if you check, don't you think?" My tone's growing more aggravated by the moment.

"There were some people around back earlier. Maybe it would be a good idea if you checked on everyone's bikes," Hammer chimes in from a booth on the side.

Fury looks at Hammer and then at me. But Jada's the one to speak. "If you're thinking about saying something like your brother did, I'd advise against it. It's not only disrespectful but dumb as hell."

Fury inhales deeply through his nose and wipes his hands on the rag he uses to wipe the bar. "All right. I'll be back in a bit. Archer, man the bar. I'm bein' sent out to do some shit you should be doing."

Archer is Chains' younger brother, a newer addition to our ranks, and our sole prospect at the moment. He got out of rehab not too long ago, and so far, the club life has been treating him well. "I told you to do it, not him," I hiss at Fury, and he doesn't say anything to me in response.

"I have a feelin' I'm gonna get shit on that for later, you know," Archer tells me with a chuckle.

"Yeah, well, they're gonna be barkin' up the wrong tree. I gave him an order, and I have rank as well as seniority. He can go fuck himself." As I speak, I notice Jada's eyes are on me, and it's a bit impossible for me not to turn and look at her.

"You want anythin' to drink?" Archer asks me.

"A Coke would be fine," I tell him, and he goes over to the soda machine. He grabs a clean glass and scoops some ice cubes into it, but as he presses down on the button for the Coke, the liquid comes out in an off-white color.

"Looks like the syrup is out. Has someone shown you how to change it?" I ask him, and he nods after a moment.

"Yeah, I'll go get a fresh bag from the stock room and change it out. Thanks," Archer tells me before walking off toward the stock room.

"Hammer, mind coming with me for a few minutes?" Breaker's voice comes out of nowhere, and Hammer gets up from the booth he's sitting in, heading off with Breaker.

It leaves Jada and me by ourselves in the bar, which hardly ever happens. I'm sure the mid-afternoon rush is going to be here any minute, so I'll soak it up while I can.

"I apologize for Fury's brashness. You were making yourself very clear to him, and he kept pushing your buttons," I tell Jada, and she laughs at my words.

"He doesn't give up, that's for certain. I, however, am not the least bit interested in ending up in his bed." Jada picks up her cup and sips on her Sprite. Not interested in his bed? She didn't say not interested in anyone's bed. I might have a shot here, but I haven't even tried to take it yet.

"The two of us haven't chatted too much. We're usually

off doing different things. I'm curious as to why you're here. Is it just to visit your brother?" I question her, and a smile tugs at the corner of her lips.

"I'm here for a visit, yes."

"Are you staying much longer?"

"I'm not sure yet. Why are you asking?"

I take a few seconds to think about how I'm going to answer her, and Jada narrows her brows at me. "We haven't had an opportunity to connect, and I'm hopeful the two of us can do that before you leave. I'm hoping you're not up and leaving tomorrow, is all." Jada and I have an intense sexual attraction to one another, and I'm certain of it. I've known it since the first time we laid eyes on one another. She couldn't stop staring at me, and I could barely keep my eyes off her as well.

The only thing is we haven't explored the chemistry brewing between us.

"I'm not leaving in the next few days, no. If I had to go back and work in an office, I would've been gone by now, but I work for myself, so I have a bit more freedom."

Interesting. "Do you have plans tonight?"

She turns her neck a bit, and her smile grows. "No, I don't."

"Great, so you'll have time to take a ride with me."

"Take a ride?" she repeats back to me, her eyes widening in the process.

"Yeah, like, on the back of my bike and stuff." I wiggle my eyebrows playfully, and Jada's frozen as she tries to process it.

She finally raises her eyebrows after a few moments. "I know it's not often that random women get to be on the back of your bikes."

"You're not a random woman, and I'm askin' you," I tell her. At first, I told her, but I didn't want to push her buttons.

She might not like that I'm so alpha, so I'll dial it back a bit right now and give her the option to say no, though I'm sure she won't.

"Fine, I'm saying yes then."

"Saying yes to what?" Hammer's voice comes back from the doorway that leads downstairs. I guess he and Breaker are already finished their chat.

"I told Armor here I was going to go shopping, and he offered to take me so I wouldn't be alone," Jada tells her brother.

"She wanted to head out near that newly renovated mall. You know the one, it's right on the outside of the rough area of town. I figured you didn't want her goin' out there by herself." It's bullshit, but I don't want Hammer to know I'm trying to fuck his sister.

"Shit, thanks, man. There was a stabbing there the other day. Did Armor tell you that?" Hammer questions his sister.

Jada shakes her head. "No, but I read about it. It was in the middle of the night, not the middle of the day. I was sure I was going to be fine, but I'm even more certain I'm going to be fine now. I doubt anyone would mess with me with this scary dude over my shoulder." Jada looks directly into my eyes, and I know we're both lying to her brother, but it's nothing serious. It's just a little white lie.

"Want to leave around four? That'll give you a couple of hours to do whatever you need, and it'll give me time to handle some things," I suggest.

"Sure, that sounds good. Thank you for offering to take me. It's very gentlemanly of you." As she says the last bit, I sense a bit of playfulness in her tone. I just hope her brother isn't picking up on it.

CHAPTER THREE

JADA

It's a few minutes before four, and I'm walking down the stairs to the bar area. Surprisingly, it's pretty packed in here. The bar's filled to the brim, except for one seat at the end. Archer is Chains' brother, and he's still manning the bar, so I lean over the end, and he walks over to me. "What're you drinkin', Jada?"

"A whiskey sour, please," I tell Archer, and he raises both of his brows in surprise.

"Sure. I'll get that whipped up for you." I find it interesting Archer left rehab, and he's working at a bar. I don't know what he went to rehab for. It might not have been alcohol, and if it isn't, it will make sense, I guess.

I take a seat on the barstool and wait patiently as Archer makes my drink. Within a couple of minutes, he's handing me the drink. I grab it and take a sip. The caramel and vanilla notes from the whiskey float over my tongue, and the lemon gives it a slight sweetness. Whiskey sours have always been my drink of choice. I kind of blame growing up in Billings for my adoration of whiskey. If there's the option of whiskey or vodka, I'll always go for the whiskey.

I'm about halfway done with the whiskey sour when a familiar dark-haired man comes walking up to me. There's a slight smirk tugging at his lips, and I smile back in return. "You needed a drink to calm down before your first ride?"

"I didn't need a drink at all. I *wanted* one. I'm not sure if you know, but there's a bit of a difference."

"Oh, you're getting a bit sassy. I kinda like it." Okay, so he's flirting with me. I wasn't too keen on Fury flirting with me, but I dig Armor. I don't know what it is about the man, but he's the physical embodiment of 'don't fuck with me'. He's the type of man who would burn down the world for the woman he loves, and that's the type of man I'm on the hunt for.

"When you insult my love for whiskey, I will get sassy. Take notes, *sweetie pie*. Whiskey is my favorite."

"Sweetie pie, huh?" Armor crosses his arms over his chest and snickers, but I think he likes our playful banter.

"Yeah, you look like you're as sweet as pie. It seems fitting, doesn't it?"

"I'd have to agree to disagree on that one, *munchkin*."

"Munchkin?" I raise both of my brows to the nickname Armor's given me.

"Yeah. It seems fitting, doesn't it?" He's throwing my words right back in my face, and it's hysterical. I finish the rest of my whiskey sour and put the empty glass on the bar for Archer when he's ready.

"Archer, I'll settle it when I come back. I doubt my tab's being closed for the day," I tell him, and Archer waves a hand in dismissal, but the next thing I know, Armor's throwing a twenty on the bar.

"I got her drink and your tip," Armor calls over to Archer as the bar gets a bit rowdier. More people are coming in through the front door, and Armor snakes a hand around my waist, leading me toward one of the doors in the back. We could go in through the storage area and straight out to the back alley, but he takes me through another doorway. This one leads out to a few steps, and we go down them. Sure enough, it's a straight shot to the back alley.

All of their bikes and cars are parked at an angle, and there's an overhang over the vehicles. I imagine it must be to shield them from rain or other weather elements. "Why don't you guys have a garage for all this?"

"In Los Angeles, it's slim pickings, so we have what we have. It works, so it doesn't bother us much."

"Don't you ever get worried someone might vandalize something or try to steal it?" I question, knowing the vehicles in front of me have to at least add up to six hundred thousand altogether.

"They'd be dead men walkin' if they ever tried such a thing. People know not to fuck with our shit. Otherwise, we'd be hunting them down, and we always find what we're looking for."

Yeah, these guys do remind me a lot of the Reapers Rejects MC, but I think the Satan's Raiders might be a bit more devious. Then again, I'm sure I don't know everything my brother or his club has been through. I'm not in the inner fold. Only the members of the club and their ol' ladies know about everything that goes on behind closed doors.

Armor walks us up to a black Harley Davidson. I don't know anything about bike styles, makes, or even really models. I can say it looks nice, and there's even a portion for someone to sit behind him. I wonder if he's ever had someone take a ride with him, but I'm not sure. Most bikers don't just let anyone on their bikes with them. From what I've heard, it's only women they're dating . . . so the fact Armor wants me to be on the back of his bike makes me a bit excited. We have chemistry, and I'm excited to explore some of it with him.

Armor grabs the leather jacket that's hanging over his handlebars and dusts it off. "It's gonna be chilly when we get outta there. You don't have your jacket on like you did earlier, so put this on."

"I was hot, so I took it off. Do I need to go get it?" In the clubhouse, it tends to get a bit warm after a while. I swear the guys here don't know what being cold even is. It's constantly around seventy-six.

"No, just wear mine. It's already here, and it's ready."

"Are you sure?" I question him, raising both of my brows in the process.

"Just wear the jacket, Jada," Armor tells me, but I still feel weird wearing it.

"You know, usually when guys do stuff like this, it means something else." I don't know if this is more than him just being a nice guy, but it very well could be. I'm not the type of woman who likes beating around the bush, so I'm trying to shoot it straight with him.

"I'm just being a gentleman, Jada. I don't want you catching a chill while we're out." Armor hands me his jacket, and I slide into it, then zip it up. His gaze stays on me for a few more minutes than I expect, and I finally look up at him.

"Did I do something wrong?"

"Nah, you just look better in it than I do," he says with a smug smirk. "Anyway, did you want to go shopping, or do you just wanna get away from here for a couple of hours?"

"I need a break. We don't need to shop at all, but I understand it's our cover story," I tell Armor and the same bit of playfulness that was in his eyes earlier today comes back.

"All right. I know just the place to take you," Armor says, and he grabs one helmet and hands it to me. I pull my hair out from the bun on the top of my head and pull my thick curls back to the base of my neck. Armor, on the other hand, goes over to some locker sort of cabinet drilled into the building and inputs an electronic key code. He grabs another helmet and puts it on his head.

He mounts the bike first and kicks up the kickstand, then I throw my leg over the bike. I've never been on a motorcycle in my life, and now I'm suddenly starting to get worried. Well, maybe I'm not worried, but I am anxious, considering this is new to me.

Armor turns the key, and the bike begins to strum to life. The entire thing vibrates, and he slides down into the alley behind the club. I wrap my arms around him, but he places his feet on the ground and stops the bike. "You're gonna have to hold onto me tighter than that, Jada." He pulls my arms around his waist tighter and then puts his hands back on the handlebars. I hold onto Armor just like he showed me.

He takes off, and the two of us weave in and out of Los Angeles traffic. We're stuck in traffic for a while, and then we get out onto CA-1, otherwise known as the coastal highway. Once we're on CA-1, we aren't in any traffic. We're simply two people riding against the wind. As he drives, I look around, taking in the magnificent view. We're so close to the ocean, and I haven't ever seen it. We're not anywhere near an ocean back home in Montana. The closest thing we have to water is a lake, stream, or river.

I don't know how long we're on the road, but eventually, Armor pulls off the interstate into a dirt parking lot of an old-fashioned diner. It reminds me of something you'd see in older movies, where the guys take the girl to get a burger and fries. It's called *Fridays*, but it's nothing like TGI. He parks the bike and shuts off the engine. I get off first, and then Armor does. We both take off our helmets and put them on the bike, then the two of us go inside.

A hostess is right at the front, and Armor tells her it's just the two of us, so she takes us across the black and white checkerboard floor and over to a red two-person booth. The two of us sit across from one another, and while Armor looks over the menu, I'm stuck looking at the interior of this place. It looks like it hasn't aged as if it was plucked from a different era.

"You two know what ya want yet?" A woman comes up with bright-red lipstick, obnoxiously chewing on bubble gum.

I can't believe she's asking us this. We just sat down a couple of minutes ago. I'm going to give her the benefit of the doubt, but she's being rude already. "We'll get two cheeseburgers with all the fixings, plus fries. Two milkshakes. One strawberry and one caramel malt. Two glasses of water would be good too."

The blonde waitress rolls her eyes. "Jeeze, you want me to kill a cow too? Gosh. I'll bring it out when I feel like it, all right, buddy?" She gets all sassy with Armor and walks away.

"What in the hell is her problem? I mean, this is her damn job," I snap, and Armor cracks up laughing.

"Fuck, I didn't tell you. Did I?"

"Uh, tell me what?"

"This joint, it's one of them diners where the entire staff is rude to you. They got some killer burgers and fries, but I get a kick out of the attitudes everyone throws on."

I've heard about these places before, but I've never, ever thought about going to one. I guess it's because I tend to get a bit hot-headed when the occasion arises. If Armor didn't tell me what this place really was, I'm sure I would've lost my shit.

"I was this," I pinch my thumb and my index finger maybe a millimeter apart, "close to losing my shit on her. You realize that, right?"

"Mmm, bet it would've been hot." I'm taken aback by Armor's remark, but I like it.

"If you say so. Now, tell me something about yourself. I'm a bit curious."

Over the next fifteen minutes, our food's brought out to us, and Armor and I talk about our lives and get to learn a bit more about each other. Though, he doesn't talk about his childhood. I even told him about the time Hammer left his cleats out in the middle of the living room, and I tripped over them, resulting in me breaking my leg. I thought our mom was going to kill him, but per usual, he got off scot-free. "Come on, you must have some sort of story like that as a kid," I joke with Armor, but his expression grows serious.

"Not really. My childhood was a bit different. It's a bit different compared to most people at the club, too."

"How so?" I inquire, waiting on Armor to tell me something else, but he doesn't, at least not yet. I think he might be a bit reserved when it comes to talking about his childhood.

"I don't think my childhood was very comparable to other people within the club. Most people were mid to lower class, whereas my family wasn't. My great-grandfather invented a lot of patents and, in turn, had a very fruitful life because of it. After that, my family kept receiving payouts, making their fortune. Because of it, I went to private school and was given the best of the best."

"Oh, wow. So, you lived a very privileged life and probably had the best education money could buy."

"Yeah, I did, but it doesn't mean my life was all rainbows and butterflies. My parents were hardly around, and when they were—specifically my father—I learned I wanted to be nothing like him. He was callous, rude, and made me feel like I was a damn nuisance to him."

"What do you mean by callous?" I think everyone has

their definition of what this means, so I'm curious to know what Armor means.

"I watched my father treat my mother like garbage. There was one occurrence I remember better than the rest. I was heading to my father's study to say goodnight to them like I always did. My mother was in the study with my father, and she asked him about a dinner party her friend was throwing. Looking back now, I think she really wanted him to go with her. She was asking him about it, not in a nagging manner, but one where she was trying to urge him. He backhanded her so hard she hit the ground, then told her he wasn't going to go."

I jolt back in my seat, shocked at what Armor's just told me.

"This is what I mean by not wanting to be a callous man."

"You couldn't be one, even if you tried to," I tell Armor, and he offers me a soft smile, almost as if it's in thanks.

Over the next few minutes, we change the subject and finish our meal. Armor ends up sharing his milkshake with me, and it's delicious. I hope we come here again because he's right, the food is amazing. Armor ends up paying for dinner, and then the two of us leave. I mentioned over dinner how I hadn't been to a beach ever, and Armor smiled widely.

We rode down CA-1 until we reached Malibu and pulled up to a beach house. Armor presses a button on the bike, and the garage door opens. He pulls the bike inside and then kicks the kickstand down. I get off the bike, and then Armor follows suit. "Is this your house?"

He gives me a curt nod, and I try not to be shocked. He owns a house in Malibu, California . . . right on the damn beach, which has to be millions of dollars. "I don't overindulge, but the things I spend my money on are homes and bikes. I have a house in Colorado as well, but I haven't been there in ages. I might as well sell it, but we don't have to talk about that. It's time to dip your toes in the water for the first time." Armor smiles widely, and I follow him into a doorway that leads to his kitchen. Then we walk through his living room to a pair of doors that lead to a deck.

We both take our shoes off and roll up our jeans to our knees, then go out on the deck. The sun's finally beginning to set, and I'm in awe of the horizon in front of me. It's a mixture of orange, yellow, pink, purple, and red.

I take a few steps closer to Armor, and his eyes are on the horizon, too, until he glances down at me. "Thank you for bringing me here, Armor. It means so much to me."

"Don't thank me yet. You haven't even felt the sand or water. Go on," he ushers me to the stairwell leading down to the beach, and I'm like a kid in a candy store. I rush down the stairs, and the moment my feet hit the sand, I'm taken aback.

The sand is warm yet so mushy. It's not like the dirt mixture we have out in Montana. The waves are a beautiful soundtrack in the background, and the water washes up on the beach. When it hits my feet, I expect the water to be cold, but it's warm.

"Is it like you imagined it would be?"

I shake my head. "No, it's better."

Armor smiles and walks within a few feet of me. I debate whether or not I'm going to do this but fuck it. He's been flirting with me. I've been flirting with him. If it goes south, it'll suck, but I'll deal with my ego taking a few shots.

I snake my hand up his chest until I'm holding onto his neck and pull his head down to me. His breath is hot on my lips, and they are only a few millimeters from touching, but not for long. I press my lips to his, and he inhales through his nose. I think he wants this kiss as badly as I do.

At least, I pray he does.

CHAPTER FOUR

Armor

I'm caught staring at her in all the beauty that she is. Her curly hair frames her face, and I'm caught staring at her plump lips. The same plump lips that are merely a few millimeters away from mine, at best. Her eyes are caught on my lips, and she looks up at me in a longing way. I think the woman is as hot as they come, but I see everything that could go bad if I get involved with her.

Then again, a lot of my brothers are finding their happiness, so maybe Jada could be mine. We've been flirty. We have a physical attraction to one another. I want to explore it, and I think she might want to do the same. So, why should we refrain from seeing where this could go?

"This is the last chance I'm giving you to walk away before we cross this line," I warn her, staring into her dark chocolate orbs.

Her lips curl up into an amused smirk. "What? Am I too much woman for you to handle?" Jada cocks a brow, and I know I'm a goner. I love her sass, her confidence, and everything I know about who she is as a person.

I plant my hands on her hips, slide them underneath her and lift her into my arms. She seems to be shocked I can pick her up without even struggling, and I walk under the house. I back Jada into one of the support beams underneath the house, closer to the back, and she sucks in a sharp breath. "Jada, let me tell you something. You could never be too much woman for me to handle."

"I don't know about that," she comments, and we both end up smirking.

Her breasts look damn good in what I imagine must be a push-up bra, and she's still in my jacket. I push her top down until I see the lace bra she's wearing and wonder if she's been in my head. It's lime green. As I trace my fingertips over the fabric, her breathing heightens. "Did you know this was my favorite color?"

"No, but I do now," she says as she bites on her bottom lip.

I want to collide my lips with hers ever so badly but fuck if I don't want to have one of these massive knockers in my mouth right now. Just thinking about is making my dick as hard as marble.

I pull the cup of her bra down, and her breast is out for me to look over. It's robust and big. I'd bet she's a double D or maybe even a triple. She's got boobs that guys like me have wet dreams over. Fuck, and she's got everything I want in a woman: a fat ass and a pair of tits she could suffocate me with.

"What if someone sees us?" Jada asks as I place my mouth over her nipple, sucking and circling my tongue against the now-hardening nub.

"Then I'll deal with them," I tell her as I rip my mouth away from the first tit. I pull the cup to the other side down and do the same damn thing. Jada arches her back against the wooden pillar and releases a soft moan, giving me every indication she likes what I'm doing to her body.

For a few minutes, I take my time with her tits until her nipples are nice and hard. She grinds her hips against mine, and I finally look up at this glorious woman. Her breathing's growing rapidly by the moment, and she's basically telling me how badly she needs to be fucked. I unbutton her jeans and pull them down, along with her matching lime-green lace thong. She helps me out by kicking off her shoes, and I throw her clothes on the sand in a pile. Luckily, the water doesn't get this high at this time of day, so I know the clothes won't get wet. I take off my cut and shirt and then remove the rest of my clothes while she takes off my jacket, her black tank top, and her bra.

Fuck, if she isn't a walking wet dream.

She has natural beauty, sure, but her massive tits and her hourglass shape, with that fat ass. And I don't mean fat in a derogatory way. All I mean is that it's plump, and goddamn if I'm not thinking about diving my face into that pussy and holding onto those cheeks for dear life.

"What?" Jada questions, almost sounding a bit nervous.

"Nothin' sweet cheeks, you just . . . you're fuckin' beautiful." Jada smiles at my words, and I manhandle her a bit. I grab her entire body and put her on the sand. She arches her back a bit, and I lick my lips, staring at her glistening pussy, and then look up at her hard nipples. With one hand, I reach up and tweak her nipples while I bring my face right against her clit. I suck the little nub, and her breathing changes yet again. Fuck, it's these little things for me.

I stop sucking on her clit and flatten out my tongue, going up and down from the entrance of her pussy to her clit. She arches her back every time I make a move, and I snicker against her glorious folds. "If you keep movin', I'm just gonna have to hold you down."

"There are no objections here," Jada mews.

Her pussy grows wetter the longer I work at it, and my

cock feels like it's gonna fall off if I don't get it wet soon. I keep lapping at Jada's wet pussy for a few more minutes, trying to show her I'm not the type of man who's selfish with this shit. But, after too long, I can't hold back anymore. I tear my face from her wet folds and go on my knees, lining my cock against her entrance.

"God damn!" Jada mutters with shock in her tone.

"Like what you see?" I ask her while I palm my thick cock. It's not long by any means, maybe a little over seven inches, but it's thick as fuck. I have the type of cock that will make a woman feel it for a couple days afterward if I fuck them real good, and I plan on Jada feeling me inside her for days to come.

"I've never fucked a white guy before, but goddamn. Your dick is so . . . fuck," she's speechless, and it cracks me up. Jada is Hammer's sister, but she doesn't have the same skin tone as he does. You can tell she's a beautiful black queen based on her luscious lips and wider nose, but her skin tone is more of a dark bronze, whereas her brother is a deep brown. I've been attracted to black girls in the past, but I've never actually been with one. I think I was always worried about cultural differences and other shit, but I know Jada and Hammer's mother was from the Caribbean, so if we end up going anywhere with this, I think they'll educate me on things.

I palm my cock as I rub the head against her pussy, gliding it against her clit for good measure. "You fucked many guys?"

Jada shakes her head, "My number is low, so I'd rather not tell you. I'm sure your body count is horrible compared to mine."

"I wanna know. I'm curious to know who else has gotten the pleasure of divin' deep into you."

Jada rolls her eyes and scoffs. "I think you wanna make

sure I'm not a ho. I slept with a guy in high school that I lost my virginity to, and we'd been dating for a hot minute. Then I slept with another guy I'd been dating back home, but we didn't work out, obviously."

"I'm glad you didn't. Then you wouldn't be here with me right now," I tell her with a wink.

I pinch her clit between my fingertips, not too hard, but enough to send her body into a frenzy. "I think you'll learn that I know what I'm doin' with a woman's body, so my body count doesn't matter. I studied, took notes, and know how to please." I lean over her, whispering it into her ear as I sink my cock deep into her folds.

Jada loses her breath as I sink into her fully, and I rock in and out of her. At first, I don't go fast. I want to slowly break her in before I wreck her pussy. She grinds her hips against me as I fuck her, and I smirk at what she's doing. Damn, she wants my cock, and she really wants it.

"Shit, I forgot to tell you I'm clean. Don't want you thinkin' I'm bein' an irresponsible asshole," I tell her as I pick up my pace. The faster I go, the more her arousal coats me. At a point, it begins dripping down my balls.

"I am too, and on the pill. I've . . . I've never had a man cum in me before, and I think it's so fucking hot. I want you to fill me up." Out of the corner of my eye, I can see Jada licking her lips, so I move my lips from her ear and capture her lips with my own. I kiss her with passion and ferociousness because I can tell it's exactly what she wants.

Over the course of maybe ten minutes, I drill my cock into her tight pussy, and her essence covers my cock and balls. I begin to tighten up and know I can't hold back any longer, and by the time her third orgasm shoots through her, her walls are constricting my cock. I can't help but release my load in her because I don't have another choice. There's no way I'd even have the opportunity to pull my dick out, not that I'd even want to.

Fucking hell, I haven't had sex like this ever, and I don't want this to be the last time, either.

I want to take her upstairs and have my way with her over and over again, and I think I just might do that.

* * *

It's about five in the morning when I wake up with Jada in my bed at the beach house. We should've gone back to the club last night because all we told Hammer was that we were going out shopping. The two of us didn't think about the consequences, but if we were lucky, he thought Jada had come back to the club and was asleep.

I grab Jada by her shoulders and delicately shake her. "*Munchkin*, we gotta get goin'."

With sleepy eyes, Jada blinks at me a few times and then grunts. Ah, she's not much of a morning person. "Come on, we gotta go before your brother kills us both. He doesn't usually get up 'til around seven, and that's how we're gonna get outta this shit." She hasn't said she doesn't want anyone to know, but I can tell the moment I mention Hammer she's a bit stressed. Jada throws the blankets off her and stands in all of her naked glory. "Fine, but I'm getting a shower quick. I'm covered in cum and sweat."

"Is that a complaint?" I ask her as she heads for the master bathroom.

She looks over her shoulder and smirks, "By no means is it a complaint. In fact, I'd much rather keep getting sweaty and cum-filled. You rocked my world last night, Armor, and I loved every second of it." Jada turns and proceeds to go to the bathroom, and within a few seconds, she disappears out of sight. She rocked my world too, and I can see myself becoming an addict with her.

Jada takes about ten minutes in the shower, and then she walks back out in a towel, dries off, and puts on the clothes she had on last night. I stare at her as she puts every article of clothing back on. Meanwhile, while she was showering, I was already dressed.

"I don't know if I have to say it, but I loved last night," Jada tells me, and warmth soars through my chest. I was hopeful she had a good time because we had a good few times last night.

"I did too. Think we should do it more often?" I arch a brow, awaiting her response.

"I do, but it can't get back to my brother or your club. I don't want any pressure on whatever this is." Jada's making a valid point.

"Fair enough. You ready to head out?"

Jada nods, and the two of us go down into the garage, get on my bike, and then we're heading down CA-1. We're at the clubhouse before six even hits, and I head in through the back first, making sure there's no one downstairs. I clear the way for Jada and help her to her room, and we share a chaste kiss before she disappears behind the door.

I'm walking down the hallway to my room when Fury comes out of his room with a brow cocked. "You're in the same shit you were wearin' yesterday, brother." I know exactly what he's doing. He's making an accusation.

"Man, I took her shoppin' then brought her back before dark, but I wasn't done. Needed to go out and get some ass. Know what I'm sayin'?" Fury laughs at what I tell him and nods. He totally understands what I'm saying.

"Gotcha. Get any decent chicks last night?" Fury's British accent comes out thicker than ever. He and his brother are both from the United Kingdom. They were in a club back home but joined the Satan's Raiders after they moved to Los Angeles. I'm not sure if I have my information correct, but I believe their mother moved out this way, which is why they moved. I don't know much about their dynamic, but I know in Chinese culture, it's very important for children to take care of their parents. I'll bet that's what they're doing here.

"Yeah, had two pawing over me. It was sweet." I flash him my playboy smile, and he cracks up.

"Any Asian girls? Chinese or Korean is what I'm lookin' for, man." Ah, now I remember. Their mother's Chinese, while their father's Korean, but he's been absent for most of their lives.

"Unfortunately, not, my man."

"Shit, I'd kill to find a good woman. It's either that or my mom's gonna set Agony and me up one day. That'll be a total disaster."

I laugh at what he's saying, and my stomach starts to growl. It's not like I didn't get any good sleep last night, so maybe I should just stay up and grab some grub while I'm at it. "I'm sure you'll find someone one day, man. I'm gonna head downstairs and get some breakfast. Catch up with you later?"

Fury nods, "Yeah, man. Sounds good."

I head down the stairwell, and the bar was completely empty a few minutes ago, but now Breaker's sitting at the bar with what looks like a whiskey on the rocks. "You good, Prez?"

"It's five o'clock somewhere, brother," Breaker tells me as he takes a sip of his drink.

It's barely six in the morning, and he's already turning to the bottle. I sit down at one of the open seats at the bar. "What's goin' on with you, man?" Breaker's been through a lot of shit since his girlfriend was the rat responsible for getting our dealers popped. He trusted that woman, and she betrayed him. I don't know if he'll ever be the same after all the shit he's been through.

"Nothin', dude."

It's bullshit. It's all bullshit. Then again, he's the one who shot her in the face after the facts were laid out. Breaker's never been violent with a woman, but he did what he would've done if a man was in her shoes. What he did would fuck with any man.

"C'mon, it's time for church," Breaker mutters and then walks downstairs.

I take the liberty of banging on everyone's doors and getting them downstairs. I call Hammer and let him know we're having church, and I'm sure Breaker's already getting in contact with Inc. Now, at least, he has the pleasure of having a time difference. It's later for his ass, so he got to sleep in a bit. After about ten minutes, everyone's downstairs, sitting in church, minus Archer since he's a prospect.

"I know it's early as fuck, but I wanted to get this shit outta the way. You all know shit has been tense since we found out Celia was the rat, feeding information to the 17. Well, they've made it known on the streets they're coming for us since our club's responsible for her death."

"It was only a matter of time before they did something," Chains speaks up, and everyone nods in agreement with him.

"Whatever those fuckers try to do, we'll be ready for them," Ice, Breaker's father and the oldest member of the club, speaks up.

"I appreciate your confidence on the matter, but regardless, this is a threat we need to take seriously," Breaker comments.

Almost everyone in the room looks over to Ops, whose ol' lady is part of the Castro cartel. The 17 are associated with cartels, so they might think we have a loophole, but I don't think we have one. I'm pretty sure Mabel was ostracized for being with Ops.

"Can your girl do anything about this, man?" Agony asks Ops.

Ops shakes his head, "No. Mabel was disowned and pretty much told she was on her own, that she wasn't a Castro anymore."

"Her father still bitter about the fact she didn't marry the guy he arranged a marriage with?" I question with amusement in my tone.

Ops nods, "Yeah, I'd say so. He's not too happy that my girl has a mind of her own."

"We'll need to deal with this threat ourselves, and I don't think we should involve any of our allies until we have to," Chains speaks up, then looks at Hammer, who's privy to being in church since he's a regent for the club.

"Chains is right. I'll take some time to think of our next course of action. Until then, be prepared. Be cautious," Breaker says and slams the gavel on the table.

We all leave church knowing war can be seen on the horizon. I just hope we're prepared for whatever comes our way.

CHAPTER FIVE

JADA

I can't describe how good it feels just to be outside in the fresh air. After taking a moment to look around the park, I realized this was exactly what I was looking for. I just want to spend some time away from all the bullshit that's going on right now. It was nice of Shiloh to get me out of the clubhouse for a while to give myself a chance to clear my head a bit. During this time, she's looking at her phone. I glance over at her from the side.

Shiloh is so good for my brother. In addition to that, she's one of the most beautiful women I have ever seen in my life, and that isn't a little thing.

The first thing I thought when I heard about her being one of the club whores was that maybe there would be some flack, but if I'm honest with myself, I believe she's the best decision that my brother could've made. I'm glad he stuck to his guns and took her on to be his woman.

Taking a deep breath and turning my head to look at the park again, I let out a sigh of relief.

"Girl, what are you even looking at?" Shiloh asks.

There's nothing particular that's happening right now. "Honestly, I'm just taking it all in and relaxing. It's truly peaceful right now."

"Peaceful? You act as though you think someone might jump out of the trees or something and come looking for us," she says.

I laugh so hard and shove my hands deep inside the pockets of my jeans. The truth is I don't want to tell her that sometimes this happens to be exactly the kind of thing I think. If it isn't that, then I believe that someone will come and harm a member of our club, or that if anything were to go wrong, the club wouldn't be able to reach the member in time.

"No, not out of the trees, but maybe from one of the cars." I shrug sheepishly, and Shiloh wraps her arm around mine.

It's been a long while since I've felt anything like a sisterly bond with anyone. I love Shiloh to death for getting me to do this.

"Don't you worry about any of that," she says, and then all of a sudden, her face gets pale, and she sways.

"Hey, you all right? Is everything okay?" I'm starting to get concerned for a minute.

"Yeah, just got a wave of dizziness. Can we sit for a minute?"

"Yeah, of course. Come on, let's go over here," I say, and she walks with me to a bench while a couple of people speedily walk by us.

I clenched up immediately, thinking this was the reason why Shiloh suddenly went pale, but the couple just kept on walking, thoroughly ignoring us. They're just out here enjoying their day like I was a few seconds ago. I'm stuck sitting on the bench, shaking my head at my paranoia.

"Girl, you just need to relax. It's fine. I think I was moving too fast. Got a little dizzy, that's all." She pats my knee and leans back against the bench, taking a few deep breaths, and the color returns to her cheeks.

I wait there for a few minutes for her to get her bearings. We weren't moving that fast. Maybe she was excited about something else. I can't tell.

She clears her throat and turns in my direction. "So, you never told me how you enjoy being in Los Angeles. What do you think so far?"

"Shiloh, if you would've told me I would enjoy being all the way over here in Los Angeles, I would have called you a bold-faced liar. This place truly is magical. It's so different from back home. If I'm being real with you, I barely miss home at all. I mean, seriously, it's not even cold here at all. I might as well have thrown away all my cold-weather clothes," I joke with her, and she joins me in a chuckle.

Halfway through, she leans forward and grabs hold of her head, and her face goes pale again.

"Hey, what's going on? You don't look good. Are you sure you're okay? Do I need to call my brother?" I put a hand on her shoulder and rub, trying my best to comfort her, even though I don't know what's going on.

"Yeah. I'm sure everything is fine. I just . . ." Shiloh takes a deep breath and leans back on the bench again. She closes her eyes and lifts her face up to the sky as if she's trying to get some air on her skin.

"Look, I don't want you to make a big deal about it," she finally says when she's able to open her eyes. "Well, scratch that. You can make a big deal if you want, but you can't tell anyone. I have a bit of a secret."

My mind goes from scared to concerned to apprehensive, then all the way back to happy. I think I know what she's going to tell me, and if that's the case, I couldn't be happier.

"What?" I bounce up and down in my seat. I'm so impatient.

"I have a confession to make, but I haven't told anyone yet," she says again and raises an eyebrow at me.

I go over everything that's happened here today and think about what it could be that would cause her to feel sick the way she is, and there's only one explanation.

"You're pregnant," I blurt out, and Shiloh's mouth drops open as she gapes.

"How did you know?" she squeaks in shock.

"Oh my god! You are?" I jump up off of the bench, and her head whips up to follow me.

"Oh wow. Okay, that was too fast." She closes her eyes again and presses a hand to her head. She's still dizzy.

"Oh, I'm sorry. Maybe we should get you back home." I sit down slowly and rub my hand over hers.

"No, I'm okay. I just haven't had anything to eat yet. When I do, I'll be right as rain." She nods slowly.

I gasp loudly, jump back up and press my hands to my hips. "You are not about to starve my niece or nephew! Let's go," I snap my fingers at her, and she laughs at my outrageousness.

"They're not starving. They're eating me up. Ugh, the doctor said it was normal, but I've already lost ten pounds. This baby is sucking me dry," she jokes, but I suddenly notice just how tired she really is.

"Come on, let's go back home anyway. You need to rest." My mind goes over what she told me earlier about no one knowing, and I wonder if that means my brother didn't know either.

"When you said no one knew, does that mean my brother's in the dark about this?" I raise one eyebrow and try not to sound too judgmental.

She bites the inside of her lip and looks away.

"Shiloh!" I say loudly.

"I'm going to tell him. I promise. More than likely today.

He's been looking at me strangely, so I'm sure he's about to find out sooner or later. I'm going to tell him tonight. I just don't want to have any argument with him. You know how he is," she says with a shrug.

"Yeah. I know exactly how he is." I nod and help her up off the bench.

My brother and I are alike in so many ways that I can almost guarantee the only argument that she's going to be having tonight is how to get him to stop tending to her. Hammer's a great father to his daughter, Oakleigh, since he found out she was his. I can't wait for him to love on this one and to actually be there for the entire experience this time.

"Oh crap, before we go home, I have to make a stop. I almost forgot." Shiloh puts a hand up to her face.

"Yeah? What for?" I ask, thinking that she's trying to get away from going back home.

"The costumes for tonight. Are you going to the Halloween party that the clubhouse is throwing?"

Oh crap, I nearly forgot all about that. I have my idea for a costume. "Yeah, I wanted to go, but I didn't pick up a costume yet. You want to head over to the costume shop a couple of blocks over that's on the way to the clubhouse?" I ask, and Shiloh nods her head. Her face has taken on her normal color, and her eyes are less glassy than before. Still, I keep my arm entwined through hers in case she falls or something like that, so I can be able to catch her.

"You're not going to let me go, are you?" she asks, and we start to walk.

"No, no, ma'am, I'm not," I say matter-of-factly and put my head up to the sky.

The Halloween store is literally only a few minutes away, and the minute we both get inside, we know what we're going to be for the party. Shiloh picked up a Sarah Sanderson costume from Hocus Pocus, and I got a circus ringmaster. Of course, both of the costumes were sexy and would be sure to turn some heads tonight. I only know of one head in particular that I want to turn, and if the way I felt in this costume was any indication, Armor's going to have such a hard time keeping his eyes off me tonight. It'll be exactly how I want it.

CHAPTER SIX

Armor

I'm sitting at the bar, minding my own business, when Hammer comes in through the front doors. There aren't any patrons in here right now, but that doesn't mean some won't be walking in a few minutes from now.

His nostrils are flaring, and I'm trying to figure out what would make him so damn irritated. "You good, man?"

"Mmm, I will be as long as all of you fuckers listen up. You better listen up real good," Hammer's voice gets louder until everyone in the clubhouse looks at him. "My baby girl is comin' into town tonight. She'll be here right in time for the Halloween party, and I swear on her life if *any* of you look at her in a sexual manner, I'll spoon out your eyes and eat them for dinner."

"*Dios Mio*, someone's being a bit dramatic," Mabel laughs in the background, and Ops glares at her to shut her mouth.

"Oh, I'm not bein' dramatic at all, sweetheart. Y'all won't even begin to understand until one of you fuckers make the grave mistake of lookin' at Oakleigh like she's your next meal," Hammer grits, glaring at every single brother in the house.

"I take it she must be a looker, then?" Killer questions and Hammer rushes up to Killer, grabs him by the collar of his shirt, and shoves him against the wall.

"My club might be allies with you, but I sure as fuck won't be if you don't heed my warning."

"Oye! Let Killer go. You know he's just busting your balls anyway." Mabel decides to be the peacekeeper here and interjects herself.

Hammer lets go of Killer, and Mabel goes into the center of the bar. "I take it everyone in here heard Hammer, yeah?"

The group of us reply to her with a series of "yeahs".

"Perfect. Don't fuck a good thing up," Mabel tells the group of us, and she doesn't need to be preaching to any of us. Hammer seems a bit heated about the whole thing, so why would we poke the bear, so to speak? We might like fucking with each other, but we're not that dumb.

A few hours end up passing by, and a lot of the brothers are in costumes. Mabel's some sort of garden fairy thing with a skirt that barely covers her ass, and Ops has been running around standing behind her. It's amusing as fuck, so I've been enjoying the show.

Shiloh and Jada came in here a while ago. Shiloh's costume looks really familiar, but I can't place it. I think she's some sort of witch, but who the hell knows. Jada, on the other hand, is a very sexy circus ringmaster, and I'd love to see her in action with that costume.

The door to the bar is open tonight, and the bar's filling up with random people from the street. Every once in a while, we do open our club to outsiders. It helps us make some good cash at the bar, too, so throwing a Halloween party was a perfect idea if you ask me.

I sit at the bar and keep staring at Jada, who's chatting

with Mabel right now. Ops comes up to the bar with an exhausted expression on his face. "You all right, brother?"

"I'd be better if my woman could wear somethin' that covers her damn ass. Fuck, I'm tired of standin' behind her the whole night. She sent me over here 'cause she thought I needed a drink to 'loosen up'," Ops grunts and leans against the bar, holding a hand up for Archer.

"Shit, is it like this every Halloween?" Archer asks as he comes up.

"Um, not sure. This is the first year we've ever thrown a party," I answer, and Archer nods.

"Doesn't matter to me. I'm gonna make a killin' in tips tonight." Archer laughs, then looks at Ops. "Pick your poison."

"Vodka, two shots," Ops answers.

Archer goes and grabs two shot glasses, then fills them to the rim with Grey Goose. Ops hands one of the shots to me while I've been nursing a couple beers.

"Dude, don't you know that saying 'Beer before liquor and you'll never be sicker. Liquor before beer, and you're in the clear.'?" Ops looks down at my beer and then raises his brows.

"I really don't give a fuck. We're supposed to be partying tonight, and you're the one acting like a chaperoning parent at prom. Drink up, buddy."

I suck it up and take the shot back, as does Ops. He then goes back over to Mabel, and Ops takes her over to a booth, sliding his woman onto his lap.

I glance around and notice Hammer's on the other side of the bar, not even facing the direction Jada's in. If I'm going to make a move, now's my opportunity to do so. I finish the rest of my beer and make my way through the crowd of people until I'm directly in front of Jada.

I grab onto Jada's hand and walk her past the bar to the

adjoining storage closet. Once we're behind the closed door, I lock it, so no one interrupts us. She pulls the string from the light hanging above us, giving us a bit of illumination.

"You certainly go after what you want. I'll give you that," she tells me, and I smirk, taking a step closer into her space. She swallows hard in anticipation, and I run my thumb against her bottom lip.

"I haven't stopped thinkin' about you since last night, *munchkin*. I've never had a woman plague my mind like the way you do."

"Is that a problem?" She cocks a brow, being a sassy little shit, but I like it.

I shake my head. "No, it's not a problem at all. If I'm bein' honest with you, I like this shit. I like the way you draw me to you. I like the storage closet and our shoppin' trip." I bring my face closer to hers until our lips are almost touching.

Jada runs her tongue along her bottom lip, "I like it too. It's hot."

"Yeah, it is." I place my hand on her hip and press my hips against her. My cock's hard and aching for her.

"We're at a party right now, Armor." There's a pressing tone in Jada's voice like she isn't down for this.

"Yeah, so we'll be quick. I need you, *munchkin*. I gotta feel you again."

"You're lucky you're cute and that you have a fat cock," Jada tells me with mischief in her eyes. She collides her lips onto mine, and I scoop her up on the table I pressed her back against. She fumbles with my belt, and unbuttons my jeans, then takes my zipper down. Meanwhile, I'm shoving her panties off to the side. Her pussy's already wet, and I know she's been aching for me all night too.

Jada palms my cock, and I drive three fingers into her pussy. Fuck, she's soaked. I pull my fingers out of her after a couple of minutes and put them in my mouth. "You taste so fucking good,"

Jada grabs me by the back of the neck and yanks me forward, crushing my lips down onto hers. She lets go of my cock and widens her legs, giving me more room to sink myself deep inside her. I move closer, so there's no distance between the two of us, and line my cock up at her entrance. It's no time before I drive myself inside her, and she wraps her legs around my hips. She leans back against the wall, and I'm thankful for the music blaring on the other side of the door.

"Fuck, Armor!" Jada cries out as I drill myself into her. I'm not being gentle in the least bit, and by the way, her eyes are rolling back in her head. I don't think it's a problem.

"You like that, huh?" I ask as I continue to fuck her like a savage.

"Yes, yes, yes. I love it. Keep, mmm," she trails off as she moans, and her essence begins to coat my cock.

"Yes, baby. Lemme feel you all over me," I whisper against her ear and then capture her lips. Her walls tighten around my cock, and then she's coming undone for me. I can barely hold myself back, but I want her to ride out this orgasm for as long as she can. I go for as long as I can until my seed is coating her inner walls.

We both stay here for a few minutes in an attempt to catch our breaths. "God, that was . . ." she murmurs.

"Damn good," I comment, and Jada smiles and nods her head.

"I think that isn't a good way to explain it, though. There have to be better words for what that just was . . . because damn." Jada goes on to compliment me, and I brush my fingertips against her face.

"You're a fuckin' vision. I hope you know that." Every word I'm telling her right now is the damn truth. She's more beautiful than most women I've seen, and while I don't know her too well yet, I'm going to bet she's just as beautiful on the inside too.

"Why, thank you. We should get back out there before people realize we're gone," Jada says, and I agree.

The two of us fix our clothes so we don't look like people who just fucked in a storage closet and then exited it. Luckily for us, everyone's too busy staring at someone in a pale pink Playboy bunny costume who just walked in through the front door. But Hammer's looking like he's going to have a stroke.

"Fuck, Oakleigh's wearing that," Jada groans, and I put the pieces together. This has to be Hammer's daughter.

I laugh, and Jada looks over at me. "He told us earlier if we so much as stared at her, he'd cut our fuckin' eyes out. And he expects no one to look at her? This is fuckin' hysterical."

Jada cocks a brow at me.

"Don't you go gettin' jealous. My eyes are on you, *munchkin*. I'm talkin' about the unspoken for men in the club."

Jada's lips curl into a smile, and then she heads over to the girl. I stick back for a minute while the two women chat, and then Jada goes up to the bar. Oakleigh speaks to her father and Shiloh, and then they're off speaking with other members of the club.

I go get another beer while I watch Jada from afar, but two masked men coming into the club causes my attention to be pulled away. They open fire on Oakleigh, and it happens in an instant. I'm pulling my gun out, and so is Breaker, shooting back at the bastards who dared to open fire in our home.

The next thing I know, a piercing scream is ringing out, and it's coming from Jada. It's like my entire world stops.

Was she hurt? Is she okay? My eyes go from her to Oakleigh, who's lying on the ground as people rush out the front doors, trying to get out of the bar. They're fucking stupid going the same way the shooters just did, but not everyone can have a damn brain, I guess.

Jada runs over to Oakleigh, drops to the ground on her knees, and I look to Breaker, who's about to have a coronary.

This was the 17. Never did I think they'd do something this drastic on the day this rumor began floating around. For fuck's sake, we all spoke about it this morning.

These bastards are going to pay for what they've done. This isn't just about planting a rat in our club anymore. They came after us in our home and hurt an innocent bystander. Only this isn't just a random woman. This is Hammer's daughter, and it makes it that much worse.

CHAPTER SEVEN

Jada

In a matter of minutes, we all went from having the time of our lives to absolute mayhem.

A loud, piercing scream echoes through the clubhouse, and it's only when I close my mouth that I realize the scream is coming from me.

I can't be seeing what I think I'm seeing.

This shit can't be happening . . . one of my greatest fears come to life.

I run over to Oakleigh as she stares at me with a look of complete shock on her face. I catch her just before she falls. The sexy bunny costume that she has on has a small hole right in the center where her stomach is, and there's red blooming out like a sick, twisted flower.

I lay her flat on the ground and hear the sound of people running around behind me, screaming for her.

"Jada, what happened? Oh my god, what happened?" my niece says, still in shock.

I press down as hard as I can on the wound in her stomach, trying to staunch some of the blood, but it's just bubbling up between my fingers.

"You're okay. Everything is okay, baby girl. Don't you worry," I tell her and pray that I'm not lying to her right now.

In the midst of my fear, anger races through my body. This is supposed to be a safe place for her. As far as I'm concerned, this is supposed to be the *one* place where I know everything is going to be okay for everyone. This shit isn't supposed to be happening, especially not in the club.

Hammer comes sliding up beside me and places his hands on top of mine, helping me to stop the bleeding as he says, "No, no, no. Oh, God, no!".

"Dad. I don't want to die. Oh, I'm scared, Daddy." Oakleigh starts hyperventilating, and tears spill down her face as fast as they fall down mine as well. I'll never get this image out of my head. When she speaks, I feel like I'm being hit by a lightning bolt, and every single word I hear from her mouth makes my body feel like it's on fire.

"There's no need to worry, baby." Hammer comforts Oakleigh by telling her, "I'm going to take care of you." Despite Hammer's best efforts, I can tell my brother's in considerable fear by the way his hands shake.

The girl we are talking about right now is his little girl. This is the little girl that he just found out about not too long ago. It was only when she was eighteen years old that she came walking into his life.

"Breaker!" Hammer yells, but Breaker is already barking out orders, telling Chains to get the car. I would offer to call the ambulance, but I know there's no way in hell we're going to sit around and wait for them to come. We need to get her to the hospital as soon as possible. She's losing so much blood.

"I didn't see it. I didn't know," Oakleigh starts to say. I can already tell she's going to start blaming herself for something that she had no control over.

I may not be able to turn back the hands of time and take the bullet out of her right now like I want to, but I can be damn sure I do everything I can to make sure she's not going to blame herself for anything.

"Baby girl, don't you do it. This isn't your fault. There's no way for you to have known that this was going to happen." I do my best to soothe her, and she cries harder.

"Hold on, baby girl. I'm here. I got you," Hammer says, and his elbows buckle as his head falls forward onto his daughter's chest. "Please, God. Please," he begs, and I want to hold my brother, but I'm too scared to move my hands from the wound.

"We need to move right now," Breaker says from behind us, and it's only then that I realize that, for the most part, everyone has been cleared out, and the door is open to the clubhouse. Chains is already in the car.

"Dad, it hurts. It hurts," she says, and her voice is so weak.

"Breaker." Hammer turns and looks up at the man who is supposed to lead the Satan's Raiders MC for an answer he doesn't have. I see tears in my brother's eyes, and I pray that it's the last I'll see. We can't lose Oakleigh now. He won't make it.

Shiloh is right behind me, and when I turn around to see her, her face is pale, and she's crying just as hard as I am. Even though she's not Oakleigh's mother, she knows how much my brother values this girl and how much her life means to him. Her love for Oakleigh is not limited to her role as a stepmother. We all love her so much. As if by magic, Oakleigh crept into all of our lives like a fucking tornado, and now that she is in our lives, we can't imagine life without her.

"Come on, man. We're ready. We need to move," Fury

says, and I realize that they're trying to get Oakleigh in the car so they can get her to the hospital.

"Hammer, brother! Look at me!" I call for him, and his eyes snap to mine. Confusion and helplessness tangled in his gaze.

"We need to get up. You guys are going to carry her to the car, so we can go to the hospital," I say, and he nods, finally understanding what we have to do.

"Oakleigh, baby girl. This is going to hurt, but just stay with us, okay? We need to move you. The boys are going to lift you up. They'll go slow." I keep my voice even, trying to be the only calm voice in the room.

"Okay. I'm ready." She takes in a few deep breaths, and I move my hand while Fury and Hammer get into position to lift her.

They raise her off the ground, and she screams out in agony. My hands dart out to help her, but I know there's nothing I can do right now. I have to let them take her away.

"Hurry up, Hammer. Hurry," I plead with him, my voice catching in my throat.

Within seconds, they're rushing her out of the clubhouse, leaving me standing there watching them. The SUV squeals off before Hammer can even get his door closed.

My entire body feels numb, and even though I can still hear Breaker yelling out orders, I can't focus on that right now. I can't focus on anything but the red blood on my hands and forearms. That's my niece's blood.

A hand lands on my shoulder, and I jump out of my daydream.

Armor.

"You okay?" he asks, and part of me wants to scream and hit him. How the fuck can I be okay right now? How can any of us be okay? We just had a madman come into our home and shoot at us. They took our safe place and made it into a war zone. I open my mouth to speak, but the words don't come out. Armor grabs me and pulls me into a hug, and I crumble into his embrace, crying my eyes out as I replay the scene of my niece getting shot over and over in my mind.

"Sssh, we got her in time, they're going to get her to the hospital, and she's going to be okay. Chains is the best driver we got. He'll get them there safely. She's going to be fine," he murmurs in my ear, and I nod at his words. They have to be true. I can't think of the possibility of it not being true.

What's going to happen to us if she doesn't make it? How we'll we bounce back from this?

He takes his shirt and wipes the blood as best he can from my hands and arms, but it's like the liquid has stained my skin. No matter how much he rubs, I can still see it there. I can still feel the warmth of it.

"They're all fuckin' dead! Come into my fuckin' house! Dead!" Breaker roars in the background, and when I look over Armor's shoulder, I see people gathering their weapons. They're going after the 17 now. They're out for blood.

Armor looks over his shoulder, and I can feel the indecision in his hold. He wants to stay here with me, but the club has work to do. They all need to be ready for what they aim to do to the 17.

"We need to go be with Oakleigh right now. Family is more important than war," I say, and even though it's not my place, I watch Breaker's eyes cloud over. Armor steps back a little bit and waits for his Prez to tell him what to do.

I'm never going to forgive myself if, God forbid, Oakleigh doesn't make it, and I'm not there for her. I know Breaker, and the rest of the people in the club feel the same way I do. They love her.

Breaker lets out a pained sigh, "She's right. We need to head to the hospital. Hammer needs us. Oakleigh too. The 17 aren't going anywhere, and even if they try to, we'll hunt them down to the ends of the Earth to make sure they pay for this. Let's go see about our girl," Breaker says and then opens his eyes to look at everyone else.

In that same instant, I rush upstairs and pull a shirt on over my costume. There's no way I can go out with all this blood on me. I don't have time to change completely, though. When I get back downstairs, the guys are already putting their weapons away and pulling up the trucks so we can all get ready to go.

I grab hold of Armor's hand, not giving a damn who sees us. We all rush to the vehicle. I need to feel Armor's hands on me in some way right now. Now that the clubhouse isn't safe, Armor is my only safe harbor right now. I need him. And when he squeezes my hand, I know he needs me just as badly as I need him.

CHAPTER EIGHT

Armor

We've been at the hospital for over six hours. Jada's fallen asleep beside me and is leaning against the corner of the wall. Killer fell asleep, and so did Sarge and Brick. Shiloh, Hammer, Breaker, and I have been awake the whole time. Agony, Fury, Archer, and Chains are all back at the clubhouse, cleaning up the mess the shooting caused. Ops and Mabel went out to a diner to get some hot coffee and food. If Jada meant nothing to me, I probably would've gone with them to get some grub. They invited most of us with them, but a few of us were asleep, or we chose to stay here with Hammer and Shiloh. Meanwhile, Ice is back home with Sunny since she's pretty late in her pregnancy.

I have to admit, Shiloh's not Oakleigh's biological mother, but from the way she's been tapping her foot and her hand's been shaking all night, you wouldn't know any different. The woman loves Hammer's daughter like she's hers, and I don't think a lot of people find that any more. It's a rarity if you ask me. Hammer has his arm draped around his woman, but the worry in his eyes is obvious.

We haven't had many updates on Oakleigh. She was rushed back to the trauma unit, and then about fifteen minutes after we got here, we were told she was being taken back into surgery to retrieve the bullet and repair whatever damage occurred. I'm not trying to be a pessimist, but part of me thinks things can't be going well. What sort of surgery lasts over six hours? It makes me think the doctors are running into problems, and they're trying to fix them. The only positive is we haven't seen a doctor come out and tell us she's dead, so there's that.

I glance over to see if Jada's stirred awake, but she's still catching some z's. A man in a white coat comes up and walks toward the group, "Can I speak to Oakleigh's parents, please?"

Shiloh and Hammer rise to their feet, and the doctor shuffles them off to a different area of the waiting room. I arch a brow, praying for not only Hammer and Shiloh but Jada that they don't have to face an unimaginable loss today.

"I hate that this shit keeps happenin' with the club. We've had enough loss, so why are we bein' subjected to more of this shit?" Breaker grumbles under his breath, barely enough for me to hear him.

"One of these days, we're going to level the playin' field with them. I think it's gonna happen sooner than you think, brother. Honestly, we're not gonna let this shit fly. We'll be here for Hammer, Oakleigh, and Shiloh right now. That's all we gotta worry about right now, bein' here for them. We can worry about the other shit later."

I catch Breaker looking at me and sense his anger growing with every passing moment. "I don't tell anyone this shit, but every night I ask myself if what I did to Celia was the right decision. I've never hurt a woman before, Armor. I don't *enjoy* the fact I made her pay with her life. I was in love with her, or rather the lie she made me believe. Was me killing her for betraying me warranted?"

Fuck, it sounds like he's had a lot of nights thinking about this. "I think you're focusing too much on the fact she was a woman. She betrayed you, yes, but she was doing far worse than that, brother. She was planted to go after you to get information for the 17. That's somethin' entirely different if you ask me. At any time, she could've told you the truth, been honest with you, but that isn't somethin' she did. Only when she was beggin' for her life did she try to get her ass out of it. The truth is, I probably would've done the same thing." I'm being as honest as I can with him, and Breaker raises both of his brows.

"I don't know if I'll ever be able to trust another woman, not after what Celia did. I stripped you all of your fuckin' patches because I thought one of you was the rat. When the rat was in my fuckin' bed. But . . . I fuckin' loved her, man, that façade she presented to me, at least. I loved that woman, and I had to make a choice."

"A choice that showed the 17 we aren't ones who can be fucked with, and that we'll take down anyone they send our way, regardless of who they are," I speak up, trying to encourage my Prez and show him his choice might not have been 'right' in a moral code, but it was the right decision for our club and the people in it.

"But is it worth it when people suffer because of it, like Hammer's daughter?" Breaker looks over to where Hammer and Shiloh are, surely blaming himself for the pain they're feeling right now.

"There are risks being affiliated or associated with the club. Everyone in it knows it. There isn't a day when we don't have any sort of risk. It might not have been Oakleigh. It could've been Jada, Mabel, or even Sunny. Hell, it could've been one of us."

"It doesn't matter, man. The point is this happened to Hammer's daughter, and maybe if I hadn't—"

"Stop your shit right there. You and I both know the 17 don't abide by any rulebook. They won't be like some other clubs who won't go after families. They don't give a flyin' fuck about the people we love, and in turn, they put their own families at risk. You did what any of us would've done, and don't overthink that shit. You were faced with an impossible decision and made one. You showed people that they can't fuck with us, and those who do will pay the ultimate sacrifice. You showed our enemies that our club isn't one to mess with." I keep trying to help Breaker see that he wasn't wrong in making the choice he did. But I don't know if he's ever going to feel good about it. I think what Celia did, the betrayal, the lies . . . I think all of it fucks with him in a way none of us will ever be able to truly understand.

A deep inhale coming from my left causes me to look over, and Jada's stirring awake. She rubs her fingers against her eyes and stretches. "Any updates?"

"Not yet. The doctor's talkin' to your brother and sister-in-law now," I tell her, and Jada lets out a sigh. I know she was hoping for another answer, but we don't have another one as of yet.

"All right. Um, well . . . I'm going to go find one of those vending machines with some coffee. I need it so bad right now," Jada says, slinging her purse over her shoulder in the process.

"I'll go with you."

Jada gives me a concerned look, probably afraid someone's going to put the pieces together between us, but I'm not worried. "Someone associated with the club was just attacked. No one is goin' anywhere by themselves."

"Okay, whatever. I can go get a coffee by myself, but if you wanna be my personal security guard, go for it." Jada dramatically rolls her eyes and puts up a fight, just on the off chance anyone's paying attention to us.

Jada starts walking in the direction of the cafeteria, and when we're out of sight of anyone from the club, I grab onto her hand. I give her a reassuring squeeze, a silent way of telling her I'm here for her because I know this woman has to be hurting.

I just hope whatever news the doctor's telling Jada and Hammer is good.

CHAPTER NINE

JADA

It feels like I've been walking in a daze for the past few hours. We're here at the hospital for Oakleigh, but none of this seems real. Armor and I went to get the group of us some snacks so we could all keep our spirits and energy up, but it all felt like a half-measure.

The minute I get back into the waiting room, I see Hammer and Shiloh holding each other.

My body goes stiff, and I'm already preparing myself for the bad news.

"No. Please, no," I whisper, and Armor rubs my back.

"Hammer?" I call out for him, and his head pops up to look at mine. He calls me over, and I walk slowly in his direction. Armor lets me go for a brief moment, and it feels like he's taken my security with him. I make my way over to Shiloh and Hammer to hear what's going on.

As much as I have never seen my brother like this, I guess I could see the reasoning behind it. His little girl is up in the hospital because of something that happened while she was in his care. It's impossible for me to imagine what he must be going through right now in terms of guilt.

"What's going on? I need to know the truth . . ." I ask, trailing off as he shakes his head in disappointment.

"No, she's still alive. The doctor has just come in and told us that Oakleigh will be okay. They've just finished the surgery, but there were complications that are still being dealt with," Shiloh exclaims at the end of his words.

"There are complications. What's happening?" I ask my brother and Shiloh, looking back and forth between them. I am dying of anticipation right now.

I care only about whether she is going to be able to make it. Since we all know she's going to be okay, our worries should be gone. That's the most important thing, after all. There must have been something significant that happened to her in order for him to be so broken up.

"While they were trying to close her wound up, the stitches kept breaking. There was just too much damage. They had to take her uterus out. It was too risky to leave it in. My little girl isn't ever going to be able to have children," Hammer says, and another tear drops from his eyes.

"Oh my God. She can't have any kids at all. This is unfathomable."

Shiloh is quick to add, "Not on her own. They took her uterus, but they left her tubes and ovaries, so she can't have kids on her own, but she may still be able to have them in other ways. It won't be natural, but she still has options," Shiloh says softly. In spite of the fact that I know she's trying to soften the blow for my niece, my heart aches so badly for her. I'm not sure what she wanted for her life, but I know that most women strive to have children at some point. At such a young age, they basically will be telling her that her chances have already been drastically reduced. It's not something that she should have to go through. Of course, I'm happy that she's going to make it, but I'm sad about the consequences.

"Okay, so what do you need? We got some food here, but what else do you need?" I reach for my brother and swipe a hand down his cheek. It is important for me to let him know he is not alone in this. We are all here to support him.

After a few breaths, he gets himself back under control, rubs the hand over the side of his face, and wipes away the tears from his eyes. "I can't leave," he says softly.

"Of course not. Do you want to be alone? Is that what you need right now?" I don't want to leave Oakleigh either, but right now, I need to make sure that my brother gets what he needs. If that means that we all have to leave him here, I'll make sure that it gets done.

"I need you to tell Armor and Breaker to go back. They can go back to the clubhouse. They need to sleep. Just send someone in a few hours with a vehicle in case we need to move. I don't want the club to be left defenseless. There's nothing more we can do right now for Oakleigh," Hammer says, and I nod my head. I can understand, but I don't want to go. Right now, it's not about me, though.

"All right, if that's what you want, we'll get it done." I turn to go back to Armor, but before I take another step, I look over at my brother. "I love you, Hammer. You know that, right?"

"Yeah, Jada. I love you too." He pulls me back into a hug, and Shiloh backs up a bit. When I'm finished, she takes my place, and I go over to where Armor and the rest of the guys are sitting, eating up the snacks that we brought for them.

"What's going on? What did the doctors say?" Armor asks the second I get over to him.

"She's going to be okay, right? It's going to be okay?" Breaker asks, and even though he's not crying, I can see the hurt in his eyes. I bet he feels somewhat responsible since this happened in his club.

"Yeah, they're just finishing up the surgery. She'll pull through." I don't feel the need to tell them about the difficulties. That's not my place.

"Hammer wants us to go on back to the clubhouse. He knows that we still have work to do, and he doesn't want the club to be left defenseless. He just needs someone to drop a vehicle back off to him in case they have to move."

"What? Are you sure? We can all stay," Breaker says, but he keeps his voice low.

"No. This is what Hammer wants. We need to give him that." My voice is strong, and even though I'm not trying to be disrespectful, I need to make sure we do what my brother asks. If I have to drag Breaker out of here myself, I will.

"All right. If that's what he wants, we'll go home." Breaker stands up and starts dishing out orders while Armor just stands by me, his energy washing over me and making me feel safe again.

I put a hand up to my mouth and let out a yawn that I didn't know I was holding in. I must be more tired than I thought.

"Yeah, we all need to get some rest. We've been burning the candle at both ends." Armor rubs a hand over my shoulder, and both Breaker and Chains shoot him a glance. No one says anything, though.

I don't have the energy to put everyone's mind at ease. I just want to get home. I nod and turn toward the door of the waiting room. I look back over at my brother one more time and silently pray that he has the strength to get through this. He needs it.

* * *

The rest of us make our way back to the clubhouse, and Breaker heads straight into his office. I expect Armor to go with him, but instead, he heads for his bedroom. I'm at a loss for what to do, and he seems to realize it. He tugs my arm for me to follow him, and I do with very little resistance. I don't want to be left by myself, and I appreciate the fact that he can sense that.

"You sure this is okay?" I ask as we walk into the bedroom.

"Yeah, it's fine," Armor answers. He closes the door behind us and runs a hand through my hair gently before he drops it. He looks down, and I see the tension in his shoulders. He clenches his jaw hard, but I can't do anything to help him right now. I just feel so numb.

"I'm going to hit the can for a minute. Relax." He points to the bed, and I nearly laugh at his choice of words. I'm so stressed out. There's no way that I'm going to be able to relax.

I've never seen this kind of violence in person. Sure, on TV and in news articles, but never right there in front of my face.

I don't know how to act or how I'm supposed to feel right now.

This is the first time I'm experiencing something like this firsthand.

I wish I had something to break me out of this.

I don't know how long Armor was in the bathroom. Time seems to be melting together. When he comes back out, he has a washcloth in his hand, and he puts it down next to me. He pushes the shirt I threw on back over my head, and when I look down, I see all the blood on my costume.

My body goes stiff, and I just want to rip it all off. Luckily, he must know that's what I want because he makes quick work of getting the offending materials off.

I shiver when he peels the costume off my body, leaving me in nothing but my fishnet stockings and underclothes.

"I'm so sorry, Jada. I'm so sorry you had to go through this," Armor whispers as he continues to take my clothes off. When I'm naked, he picks up the washcloth and starts to wipe off any remnants of blood.

"I was so scared. I think I still might be scared," I finally whisper, and he drops the washcloth to the side.

"No, babe. You don't need to be scared anymore. I'm here. I'm always going to be here to protect you, Jada," he whispers and kisses me.

These aren't the needy passion-fueled kisses that we usually share, instead, they are sensual and loving.

He's pouring all he has into the kiss, and I'm soaking it up. Slowly, the feeling of numbness leaves my body, and all I want is him.

I tug at his clothing, and he's quick to take them off. He lays me back on the bed and slowly kisses my body, taking his time to let me feel him.

He runs his hands softly down my core and slides his fingers between my pussy lips. My body reacts violently to the touch.

I want more of this. More of him.

I arch up into his expert hand, and he slowly pushes one finger and then another inside of me.

"I need you, Armor," I whisper, and he grunts in response.

His cock is hard and ready for me. He slides his knees between my legs to open me up more. I take advantage of the situation and wrap my legs around his waist.

He thrusts slowly inside of me, and I let my eyes flutter closed.

All the pain and agony of the past few days float away as he rocks my body. The deeper in me he is, the more at ease I feel.

My orgasm is slowly building, and when I release, he captures my moans in his mouth.

The things this man makes me feel.

Armor rocks my body for hours until I'm sated, and even though I'm still worried about Oakleigh, I know undoubtedly, I'm going to be safe in Armor's arms.

CHAPTER TEN

Armor

Being with Jada has caused me to not be as focused on a lot of my business outside of the club. I still haven't told anyone besides Hammer and Inc about what I do with my money but being with Jada makes me question if one day I can tell her about it. She's becoming more important to me as the days pass, but I'm not sure she's ready to see the reality of this cruel world.

A lot of people act like it doesn't exist, or they choose to not see it for what it is: foul. I, on the other hand, have never been the type who could ever turn a blind eye to this sort of shit. I think growing up the way I did only made me see it more. I witnessed how the rich would speak to the people who worked for them. The very people who would clean their houses or make their food. They'd act as if they were below them just because of the nature of their jobs.

As a child who bore witness to it constantly, it made me understand there were two types of people in this world: the good and the ugly. I was just trying to understand it back then, but my father and people like him were the ugly. The people helping them, doing their jobs, aiding them . . . those were the good people, though they often chose to not see that.

I think it all adds up to why I don't work with my father or his associates. I didn't want to act like some sort of pompous asshole. It's never been in my nature, honestly. I even turned down a six-figure-a-year job at one of my father's companies. He didn't understand it, but I already had a trust fund to live off, and it would provide for me, my future wife, and any children I had quite handsomely. Add in the fact I've invested some of it and donated a bit more, then I take the kids out of trafficking. I don't live over my means, though. For example, I'm the man who will eat ramen just to save a few extra bucks. I don't need lobster and steak every night. Those sorts of meals are for important things, not minuscule overindulgences just because I can.

It's been a few days since Oakleigh was taken to the hospital, and the fact it's November blows my mind. If anything, it feels like this year has flown by. Since she was shot, the club's been having people on the streets contacting our dealers, and we've been taking shifts watching over the perimeter of the club. The fact the 17 came in here and opened fire is complete and utter bullshit. They have no regard for keeping family or loved ones out of harm's way, but we won't play as dirty as they do. We'd never put an innocent woman or child in the crossfire just to get back at our enemy.

I'm sitting at the bar, and Jada's upstairs. She told me she wanted to take a hot shower, so I'm down here having a drink. My mind keeps replaying everything that's happened over the last few days, and the more I think about the series of events, the more I get frustrated. Could we have stopped them from coming into the club? Should we have had people posted at the door? There are so many what-ifs running through my mind, but I know it has to be worse for Hammer. His child's the one still at the hospital, and she'll likely be there for a couple more weeks. He's been telling us how she has some sort of physical therapy she's already started. I don't pay too much attention to the details because there are so many other things on my mind.

I'm supposed to be meeting with one of Otis' contacts in a couple of days. His name's José, and I'm told Jose can help me get access to information I want, such as other traffickers higher up the ladder.

I take a sip of my drink, and my mind continues to mull around. I'll always wonder what we could've done differently to avoid bloodshed, but the fact of the matter is that if we had let Celia live, the blood might not have been spilled in the first place. I don't blame Breaker for what he did. Not in the least bit. I would've likely done the same if I had been betrayed in such a way. The 17 crossed the line when they sent Celia here, and the cartels associated with them as well.

Ops' woman, Mabel, is tied to the Castro cartel . . . but she's been pretty much disowned since she's chosen to stay with Ops. Her father won't help her, or us by extension. We're left to deal with this mess ourselves, and at the end of the day, I know we'll handle it however we need to. All I can hope for is that no one else we love gets hurt in the process.

"You want another?" Archer asks as he makes his way down the bar, checking on club members and patrons.

I shake my head. "No, but thank you."

Between the attack on the club, doing the shit I do on the side, and my growing . . . whatever I'm doing with Jada, I'm spent. We're still keeping it a secret from everyone, and I'm all right with that, but she's made a couple of remarks to me that she wants to stay in Los Angeles . . . so could this turn into something different? I think so.

I think I could end up wanting to be with her long term,

and the more I think about it, the more I can see her being my ol' lady. She's dropped a couple hints that she doesn't want to keep lying to her brother or rather hiding us. I haven't told her not to speak to Hammer because the fact of the matter is I don't want to hide her. She deserves a man who will walk in the light with her, and I want to be that man.

All I can hope for is that she doesn't change her mind about staying here in Los Angeles.

CHAPTER ELEVEN

JADA

This is about to be the most nerve-wracking conversation I'm ever going to have in my life.

It's time to end all the secrets and sneaking around. I'm too old to be doing this, and the more that it happens, the more I feel like I'm double-crossing my brother because I know I'm only doing it because I feel like he wouldn't approve.

These feelings that I have for Armor aren't going away. In fact, they only seem to be getting stronger. After all that's happened over the past few days, I don't need to be concerned about Hammer worrying about me. He deserves to have all of his attention focused on Oakleigh and Shiloh.

I know for him to do that, I need to come clean about what's really going on with Armor and me.

Hammer and Shiloh are supposed to be on their way back from the store, picking up a few more things for Oakleigh. I pace back and forth in front of the doorway to catch him before I lose my nerve. If I have to wait for tomorrow or even later today, I don't know if I'm going to be able to go through with it.

My heart stops and then skips a few beats when I hear Hammer's truck pull up in the alleyway.

It's now or never.

I grab hold of the door and walk out in clear sight where he can see me. The minute he steps out of the car and sees me standing there, his expression drops into a scowl.

"What's going on? Is everything okay?"

"Yes, everything is fine. I need to talk to you," I tell him and cross my hands over my chest. I squeeze my biceps, trying to draw strength from anywhere inside myself. I wish Armor was here right now with me, but I'm not doing this for his permission. I'm doing this for myself.

Hammer's eyebrows furrow as he comes closer to me, the bags in his hands and Shiloh at his side.

"Okay, give me a few minutes to put this stuff down, and we'll talk," he says, and I shake my head no before I step in front of him. "No, I need to talk to you now. It's important," I tell him, and Shiloh reaches over for the bags.

"Go on, you two chat. I'll take these inside."

I worry for a second that the bags might be heavy, and she shouldn't be carrying them, but she's already gone before I can say anything to her.

"Okay, you got me out here alone. What's so important that it couldn't wait a few minutes?"

I had an entire speech planned for him, but now that he's standing right in front of me, I can't think of anything I wanted to say besides the fact that Armor and I are together.

I start with the few things I know the answers to. Hopefully, that will put him on a path where he has no choice but to see that everything will be okay with my choices.

"Hammer, do you trust this club with your life?"

"What the fuck? What kind of fucking question is that?" he asks, instantly getting his feathers all ruffled.

"Humor me," I say, rolling my eyes quickly.

"Yeah, of course, I trust them with my life. They'd do everything in their power to protect me. I might not be a Satan's Raider, but as a regent for the Reapers Rejects, we all protect each other."

I nod. I already knew he'd say that. "What about me? Would you trust them with my life?"

"Yes, of course."

I nod again, moving right on to the next question, "How about me? Do you think I'm smart enough to make good decisions? You trust me to know what's good for my life?" This one I'm not so sure of the answer.

"Well, I mean, yeah, you've grown up all right. I know you can take care of yourself and will come get me if anything is too hard for you to handle."

That's what's about to change. It's no longer him that I'm going to go to, but Armor.

"Good, that's what I thought. I've made a decision and I know you're not going to like it. But just know the only reason I know this will be okay is that I know that you and the rest of the men in this club will do everything to keep me safe. I know that through you, I've become family. I know that there are no other people on this planet who will treasure me and treat me better than you guys."

He shoves his hands in his back pockets and tilts his head to the side, not understanding what it is I'm talking about.

I take a deep breath and make sure I keep his gaze. If he thinks I'm unsure about this at all, I know it's going to be that much harder to convince him.

"Hammer, Armor and I are together, and I'm going to stay in Los Angeles indefinitely." The words seem to echo in the air, and my brother stares at me with wide eyes.

"What the fuck did you just say to me?"

"I'm sorry, it's not something I meant to happen, but it did. We care for each other a lot. The man would rather walk on hot coals barefoot than go against your word, but we can't help how we feel about each other. I love him, and I'm going to stay here to be with him."

"The fuck you are. You're going back home," Hammer says and tries to walk around me to the clubhouse doors.

"Hammer!" I grab hold of his arm, stopping him from moving. "You just told me that you trusted this club with your life and mine, so why is it when one of them is offering to protect my heart as well, you have a problem with it? You know Armor. You know what kind of man he is. I wouldn't be here telling you this if the man treated me any less than a queen."

"For fuck's sake. It's not about Armor. I know he's a good man, and he's going to do right by you. He knows I'll knock his fuckin' teeth down his throat if he doesn't. That's not the problem."

I throw my hands in the air, exasperated. "What the hell is the problem then?"

"This life! This life and having you in it is the problem!" he yells.

He lets his hands fall to his sides and takes a deep breath before he continues, "Jada, you don't deserve to be in this life."

Ah, that's what this is about. "Oh, come on, it's not that bad."

"Don't be stupid. You're talking to someone who's been living it for years. I know exactly how bad this is. You need to go back home where this shit can't touch you."

"I already told you I made my decision, Hammer. I appreciate the brotherly concern, but with your approval or not, I'm staying." I put my hands on my hips, standing my ground.

"How can you want to be around this? Were you not there when your niece was gunned down like livestock? Did you not see those bastards who tried to roll in here and kill us while we were supposed to be having a good time? Don't you realize the dangers that go along with being attached to a high-ranking member of this motorcycle club? The minute you become Armor's ol' lady, you're going to have a target on your back. You think I want that for you?"

"No, I know you don't, but I think you do want me to be happy and be with someone who cares for me enough to keep me that way."

I reach over and put a hand on his arm. No one could ever tell me that my brother doesn't care for me. I know he's been traumatized by everything that's been going on with his daughter, but I can't let that event stop my life.

He snatches his arm away from me and puts both his hands up.

"Fine, it seems like no matter what I say, you're going to go about doing this your way. I don't even know why you came to me with this shit in the first place. Do what the hell you want. I'm out of here." He turns and storms off to his truck.

He puts it into reverse and drives out like he's running from the cops. I feel bad that I've hurt his feelings, but I'm happy that it's finally out in the open. I am slightly worried that he may try to distance himself from me. That's just my brother's way. He can hold a grudge like no other. I make a note to talk to Shiloh about it when I have a free moment, but right now, I just want to bask in the feeling of being free. Free to love who I want, kiss who I want, and not have to hide in the closet to do it.

I turn to walk back into the clubhouse and find Armor. He's the next person I have to tell my plans to, especially since they majorly involve him.

He might have had an idea that I was getting ready to spill the beans to my brother, but I don't think he knew that I was going to be moving here as well.

I don't see Shiloh when I walk in, but I do see Agony and Fury sitting at the bar.

"Jada, everything good with Hammer?" Fury asks.

"Yeah, he's mad at me. He'll be back when he cools off."

He leaves it at that and turns back to talk to Agony.

I rush up to the back rooms where I know Armor is.

I open the door just as he's coming out of the shower. I'm slightly distracted by the fact that he's naked, save for a towel around his waist.

God, my man is sexy as fuck.

"You're doing a lot of gawking over there. We need to find a closet?" he jokes, and I feel a big smile push up my cheeks.

"Not anymore," I say, and his eyes focus like lasers on me.

"What?"

I rush and sit on the bed, patting the side next to me, so he can join me. I grab hold of his hands and get ready to lay everything that went down on him.

"I told Hammer. He knows that we're together."

He pulls back slightly, his body going a bit rigid. "Shit. I'm going to die today, then."

"No, he's not upset that it's you I chose to be with."

"He is upset, though?" he asks, and I nod.

"He's upset that I'm going to stay in this life. He doesn't want me around all this. The problem with that excuse is he already told me he knows that you and the rest of the members of the club will protect me with their lives. So, if here's where I'm going to have the best protection, why in the hell would I leave?" I shrug and chuckle slightly.

"So, it's really okay. I can have you all to myself?" Armor

asks, his pupils dilating with desire as he threads his fingers through my hair.

"Yes, we can be together." I lean forward to kiss him but jerk back when I realize I haven't told him the other part of my plan.

"Wait, there's more."

"What?"

"Like I said, there's no reason for me to leave, so I've decided that I want to stay here in Los Angeles indefinitely."

His eyes go wide, and suddenly, I feel the need to backpedal. "I can find my own place, so I'm not suffocating you or whatever."

"Absolutely not. You stay with me. I want you to stay here too. I just didn't know if going back home was something you'd be willing to give up," he says before he brings his mouth back to mine to finish the kiss I stopped earlier.

It's at that moment that I truly feel how much Armor values me. His lips on mine make me feel all warm on the inside. Not just because he's a damn good kisser but because I know I can have this anytime I want.

"Let's go downstairs. I'm excited to show off my new man."

"I'm not new. I'm just the same old me," Armor says, kissing me one final time before he gets up and puts his clothes on.

We walk out hand in hand without a care in the world. When I went into Armor's room, there were only two people out front, but now several more people were there at the bar, including Shiloh.

Fury is the first one to spot us, and his eyes instantly drop to our still-entwined hands.

"Oh, so this is what the fuck is going on now?" he asks loudly, causing everyone to turn and look at what he's talking about.

"Shit!"

"Hammer's going to kill him."

"I knew it!"

Shiloh is the one to say the last comment.

Armor pulls me closer and drapes an arm over my shoulder. "Yeah, this is what's going on. Hammer gave the okay . . ." Armor looks at me for confirmation, and I nod, "Jada's my woman."

I want to jump up and down, punching my fist in the air because I feel like I've just won a great victory.

"Well, as long as you got the go-ahead, I think that shit rocks. Come on, get a drink." Breaker waves us over, and the two of us sit at the bar together.

Everything goes on, as usual, no one really paying us any mind, but I feel like a live wire.

Once I get my drink, I calm down a bit. I didn't realize just how stressed I was on top of being happy to be out in the open.

"God, that's good. This was stressful," I mutter over to Armor.

"Tell me about it. I'm sorry you've been through all this just to be with me. How about, to make it up to you, we go on a real date tomorrow? Now that we're out for the world to see, there's no reason to hide."

"You want to take me on a date?" I ask, smiling wide again.

"Abso-fucking-lutely." He leans forward and kisses me softly.

I lose myself against his lips, and it's only when I hear the embarrassing 'awww' coming from everyone sitting around us do I realize that we truly are outside our little bubble. Now our happiness can be shared with everyone around us.

CHAPTER TWELVE

ARMOR

Jada's staying in Los Angeles permanently. She told me yesterday. I thought for a while that she'd end up changing her mind. I didn't want her to, but deep down, I kept telling myself she'd decide one day that she didn't like it here. Fortunately for me, that wasn't the case. Last night I told her we'd go out this evening for a date.

This morning she told me about a show she wanted to see at the theatre. I haven't been to a theatre since I was a small boy, and it was something my mother and father typically forced me to go to. I hated it back then because I found the subject matter boring, but I think the stuffy tux I was forced to wear didn't help. Then again, I was a child. I suppose anything your parents want you to do when you're a child isn't necessarily fun. I'm excited to be going with Jada, but I'm not very excited to be going to the theatre. But, because of the way I feel for her, I'd probably do anything, maybe even walk on hot coals barefoot.

I've been buying enough product from Otis that he got me in contact with a man named José. José is also a trafficker contact in the Southern California region, but José has quite a few international brokers. The plan today is that I'm meeting one of José's contacts. His name is Vik, so I'm assuming he's a Russian broker, but I won't know until the motherfucker actually shows up.

I keep glancing at my phone because I need to meet Jada in forty-five minutes if we're going to make it to the theatre at a decent time. The only decent thing is that I was smart enough to shave up a bit to look a bit more clean-cut and change into a suit. I drove one of the club's grocery getters out here, and I'm in a parking lot at an old industrial park. Not even one-third of the buildings are rented out, and it's after hours, so most of the people are gone by now.

I'm sitting in the blacked-out SUV, waiting for anyone to show up. I keep looking down at my phone, and before I know it, another ten minutes have gone by. Shit, now I have a little over half an hour to get back to the club and take Jada out.

I sit back in my seat and wait because it's all I can do. Jada didn't just tell me she was staying in Los Angeles permanently. No, she dropped another bomb on me. She told her brother that the two of us were together. We didn't even discuss an official term for us, like if we're dating, boyfriend/girlfriend, or whatever. I didn't even care that she told Hammer we were together because it damn well feels like we've been this way for a long time.

Jada is unlike any other woman I've been with before. In a way, I think that should be frightening, that she's unlike any other . . . but instead, it excites me. She's as gentle as a lamb but as fierce as a lion. It's probably why I can see myself being with her for many years to come, if not for the rest of my life.

I continue to look around the parking lot, and I'm disappointed as more minutes pass by. In all honesty, I'm growing aggravated. José told me they'd be here at a specific time, and neither one of them had shown up. How can someone do business and not have the decency of being on time with their potential client?

Just as the thought runs through my mind, a set of headlights come down in the direction I'm parked in. I can't tell the make or model of the vehicle because half the streetlights here don't work. I imagine when only a third of your industrial park is rented out, you can't afford to keep up with all of the basic maintenance.

Finally, the vehicle pulls a few spaces away from mine. The driver gets out first, and then the passenger. The passenger comes around to the driver's side, and I get out of my vehicle, leaving my keys inside in case I have to get out of here quickly.

"Otis speaks very highly of you," a man with a thick accent states, who I naturally assume must be Vik.

"As he should. I'm one of his best clients," I tell him, and then I glance over at José, who I'm planning on doing business with now as well.

"So he says," José pipes up and then clears his throat. "This is Vik, the other supplier I was informing you about."

I glance down at my Rolex and look at the time. "You have fifteen minutes to sell me, so I suggest you make it quick."

"Fifteen minutes, is that all?" Vik laughs boldly.

I look right at him at clench my jaw. "I was the one who was here when our meeting started. What's your excuse?"

"We were held up by another client."

"A shitty excuse if you ask me. I'm here with deep pockets and plan on doing a lot of business with the two of you, yet you disrespect me by being late. Why should I do business with the two of you now? Hmm?" I question, allowing my tone to grow aggravated. I want them to know I'm pissed about them not being here when they said. I want them to think they have a shot at losing me as a client and every bit of business I could pass along to them. The reality is I'm not pissed because they're late. If it were any other day, I probably wouldn't give a fuck, but I give a fuck because I have plans with Jada. The last thing I want to do is disappoint her.

"Because you won't find product like what I sell anywhere in the United States. Unlike my colleagues, the ones I sell aren't wild. Mine are trained in every aspect of what you or your customers could need from them. Trained to obey, to please, and to make sure you're happy with them. My girls are under the impression that if they do as they're told, their lives will be very easy. They've learned when they disobey ... that is when punishment will come down on them," Vik says, and I look over to José.

"What of your product, José? Are they as well trained as Vik's?"

José doesn't even take a moment to shake his head. "No, not all of them. I work here with Vik to give him a certain supply of my girls. He then takes them and puts them into his training program. At which point, those are the best of the best. I can still get you certain types of girls quickly, but they won't be as accommodating as Vik's. If you want to find women who will do as you ask, whenever you ask them, those are Vik's. I figured you might want to sample a few of them, which is why I pitched bringing Vik to this meeting."

"I see. How much are your girls?" I question Vik, who's quick to answer me.

"Triple what you pay Otis."

I raise my brows. "That's steep. Don't you think?"

He scoffs and then shakes his head. "No, I don't. Not when it comes to perfection, and that's what my girls are —perfect."

"I like the ones who have fight in them," I tell both of the men, and I notice José standing up a little taller. Right now, he's probably thinking he's getting all of my business.

Vik waits a few moments and then laughs. "In the beginning, I enjoyed them too, but after a while, it becomes frustrating when they disobey you. Now I enjoy *breaking* them."

"I don't know how you could miss the fight they have in them. When they obey all of the time, don't you find it a bit boring?" I question Vik, and his lips curl into a smile.

"Come with us. One of my facilities isn't too far away. If you see the product yourself, you'll understand why they're so good," Vik tells me, and I glance down at my watch. It's already been fifteen minutes, and I'm going to be late. But he's taking me to one of his facilities, which is huge.

I could bring this location down when I'm ready to strike, and I'm damn well ready to do so.

CHAPTER THIRTEEN

JADA

I'm going to fucking murder him.

I open and close my hands, trying to get the feeling of rage to ease from my body, but no matter what I do, I can't calm myself down. I can't believe Armor would leave me hanging like this. He knew how much this shit meant to me. He knew that I was going to be here waiting for him, but here I sat thirty minutes after we were supposed to leave, and I hadn't heard a word from him or anyone else to let me know that he was going to be late or whatever.

I'm so fucking pissed.

"That's what you get for trusting that he was going to stay to his word," I whisper to myself, and I look back over at the clock. The time hasn't changed from what it was before, but still, enough time has passed for me to know that I'm not going to sit around and wait for his ass any longer than I already have.

Considering all the things we've been through over the last few days, it seems as if Armor's determined to prove to me that he's just like a lot of the other guys out there. There's no time for me to deal with the bullshit.

Pulling out my jacket from the closet, I slip it over my shoulders before going to grab my purse and walk out of the room. The unshed tears in my eyes are blurring my vision, but I don't want to ruin my makeup, so I look up to try and get them to go away as fast as possible. He's not worth the mascara smears.

* * *

My eyes were glued to my phone for the entire first half of the show, waiting to see if any message would come through from Armor, and just as I had anticipated, nothing ever came through. My emotions swung between pissed off and worried and then right back to pissed off again. My first instinct is to call one of the other club members, but this isn't something they should be dealing with. There is no doubt that Armor would find a way to get in touch with me if he wanted to talk to me. Despite doing my best to enjoy the show, I've already hit rock bottom as far as my mood is concerned.

In fact, by the time they've called intermission, I'm so enraged that I have no idea what the show is about at all. I'm not paying attention.

I get outside, and just as I suck in a deep lungful of clear air, I hear the sound of a motorcycle roaring down the block.

When Armor parks and hops off his bike, I want to laugh, that is, before I have the feral need to kill this bastard.

"You've got to be kidding me," I say as he rushes over to me.

"I'm sorry, there was traffic," he offers up as an excuse.

"Traffic? Fucking traffic, Armor?" I cross my arms over

my chest, not wanting to give him any indication that I want his hands on me right now. Not the way I'm feeling.

"Jada, I'm not sure what you want me to say. There was traffic. I tried to get here." He shrugs as if that's enough of an answer for him not to take the plans that we had seriously in the first place. I refuse to just let this shit be swept under the rug. If I'm going to be with him, I need to know that I have some sort of priority in his life, and this bullshit about there being traffic isn't showing me that.

"Armor, I don't know who the hell you think you're talking to, but you can take that bullshit excuse and leave. There's not that much fucking traffic in the world that would've kept you from picking up the fucking phone and letting me know what the hell was going on."

Armor flinches backward and cocks his eyebrows upwards as I step into his space even closer. If he thinks this is going to intimidate me right now, then he's out of his mind. "Be careful, Jada."

"Careful? No, the one that needs to be careful is you." I poke him hard in the chest, desperately trying to evoke a response from him.

"You knew what the hell we had planned. You knew it was important. You made your choice to be wherever or with whoever you chose to be with. If I'm going to be last on your fucking list of shit to do, then I don't want to be on the list." I flip my hand and try to turn away from him to go back into the theater.

He grabs my arm hard and turns me to look at him. "What the fuck is that supposed to mean? Be straight with your shit, Jada." He glares at me. He wants me to spell it out for him. Fine, I can do that.

"Be straight? Fine. I don't know where you went, but I know over the past few days, you've been acting shady as fuck. You're throwing up red flags all over the place, and everything in my body is screaming that you're two-timing me," I say, getting exactly what I feel out of my mouth.

His eyes go wide, as does his mouth for a second as he fights for something to say.

Finally, he comes back with, "Jada, I don't know how we got here, but this isn't what it looks like."

"No? Then prove it, Armor. If you want me to believe that you're on the same page as I am with this fucked up relationship, then you're going to have to put your money where your mouth is and prove this shit to me."

"How the fuck am I supposed to do that?" He lets out a hard breath and runs his hands through his dark hair. "Look, I know shit has been fucked up lately, but I'm not fucking around. You're a priority to me. I just had some business to handle." Now it's gone from traffic to business to handle. I scoff and shrug my shoulders. Nothing he's saying right now is putting my mind at ease. In fact, the more it doesn't add up, the worse I feel. I'm just as pissed off as I was moments ago. I see everyone else walking back into the theater, and I know it's time for the second half of the show to start. I don't have the energy to sit through it. My mind isn't here right now.

"Jada, I promise you it's not what you're thinking."

"I've already told you what you need to do. If you can't, there's no need for you to say another word to me." I glare at him, daring him with my eyes to keep up his excuses. He doesn't say anything. Instead, he just glares at me the same way I'm doing at him.

"Fuck it. I'm going to tell you what I was doing since you need to know so badly. I have a trust fund. Just some money left to me. We've been hearing rumors about some fucked up shit going on. The club is doing what it can about the situation, but I know with that money, I can do more. I've been using it to find and help kids who are in trafficking situations. They need the funds more than I do, and I have no problem making sure that they get what they need," he says, and it's my turn to stare at him with a gaping mouth.

Out of all the shit he could have said, that's not something I would have expected him to come out with.

None of this shit makes sense. Why wouldn't he just tell me this before? Where did this trust fund come from, and why today, out of all days, did he feel the need to handle this business?

No, something seems off with this. He's lying to me again.

"No way. You can't just drop this on me with nothing to back it up." I put my hands on my hips and squint my eyes at him. I'm going to need more than his words for me to believe this shit.

"Fucking hell, woman." Armor reaches into his pocket and pulls out his phone. He dials a number and puts the phone on speaker.

I look around again and see that he and I are the only ones still outside. Everyone else has gone in.

"Brother?" a man answers.

"Inc, I know this goes against protocol, but I'm standing here with my woman who seems to think she needs some proof as to what I was doing before I came to meet with her. Can you please explain to her what I just left?"

I stand frozen in disbelief as Inc tells me all about the trafficking kids and how there was a problem today while Armor was going to pick up a few of them. They were really doing what Armor had just said.

The anger that has been flowing through my body slowly starts to ebb, but it doesn't disappear completely. Of all the excuses, this is probably the one that I can accept the most. Still, he could've called me. He should have known that I was going to be okay with something like this.

My body feels drained from the emotional rollercoaster I

just went through. Now all I want to do is go home and go to sleep. So much for getting to this show.

I sigh and thank Inc for the explanation before Armor checks in with him again and hangs up the phone.

"You want to go home?" he asks, his voice tight, and his fingers hold his lid in a vice grip.

"Yeah. I'm done," I say and start to walk off. He grabs my arm and pulls me over to my truck.

"What about your bike?" I ask.

"I'll come back for it," he replies before he gets into the front seat and waits for me to get in and buckle up.

The tension between us is thick, and after Inc explained everything to me, Armor hasn't said more than a few words. We're both mad at each other, but right now, I don't care about how he's feeling. I didn't leave myself in the dark about this.

When we get back to the clubhouse, no one is there. The last I heard, they were going to go down to the bar.

I figure that Armor's going to join them as I go upstairs for a nap, but he grabs my hand and pulls me up to his room.

The minute the door closes, he pushes me hard against the wood.

I'm shocked that he's being so rough with me, but I know deep down that he'd never physically harm me. Emotionally and mentally, I'm not so sure.

"Another bitch? You think I'm fuckin' around with another bitch?" He threads his fingers into my hair, and a few of the pins fall out.

"What do you expect? You don't tell me anything," I snarl at him.

"I shouldn't have to tell you shit. You know you're all I fuckin' want, Jada. Nothing should make you doubt that shit. Ever," he snarls back.

"You don't show me . . . I don't know." My confusion

ramps up, and instead of the anger I'm feeling, it turns to blind need.

"I'll show you . . .I'll show you every fuckin' minute of the day if you need. You're mine. I don't want anyone else but you," he snaps before he slams his lips down to mine in a bruising kiss.

I grab hold of his head and neck and dig my nails into the skin, which just makes him push against me harder. I kick my shoes off and lift one leg so I can get closer to him.

Fuck, I need this man more than I want my next breath.

I'm wearing a tight skirt, and when he raises my leg higher, I hear it tear. I push him away hard, and he stumbles backward in shock. I'm not telling him no but getting right to the business. I yank my top off, leaving the chunky ornate necklace I'm wearing on.

"God damn it, girl. How could I even look at another woman when I have you?" he groans and reaches down to palm his cock through his pants.

The jean fabric is tenting, and I know he's in pain.

Good. He should hurt a little after what he did to me today.

He takes his cut and shirt off, tossing them on the bed as his eyes continue to rake over my body. I slide my torn skirt off and stand in front of him in only my thigh-highs, bra, and panties.

His breaths are ragged as well as mine. I reach forward, and he quickly moves into my grasp. I turn, so he's the one against the door this time.

He grabs the back of my neck and tips my head up, so he can kiss me again. While he's sucking and nipping at my mouth and neck, I rush to get his pants down.

I don't wait for him to step out of them before I'm on my knees in front of him. He says he's mine. I want to taste him.

When I pull his long, thick shaft out of his boxers, he

growls deep in his chest. "Sexy as fuck. I'm a lucky son of a bitch."

"Tell me about it," I reply a second before I open my mouth and suck the head of his dick in between my lips.

"Fuck!" He slams his head back, and I quickly get to work, trying to get him as deep into my mouth as I can. I use my hand to jerk the part of his shaft that I can't get in yet. I suck him hard and pump my mouth quickly, pushing him closer to the edge. I want him to feel as crazed as he makes me feel.

"Jada. Fuck, stop," he groans, but he uses his hands on either side of my head to help me take him deeper.

"Mmm," I moan and ignore his request.

My inner sex kitten purrs when I feel his knees go weak. I love that I can get him this way.

"I'm not going to bust in your mouth. Fuck, I'm not," he says more to himself than to me. As much as I want to prove him wrong, I don't want him to finish there, either.

I pull his throbbing cock out of my mouth with a loud pop, "Where are you going to come then, Armor? You going to make being late up to me? You going to give me all you got?" I say in a whisper, looking up at him from my knees.

"Fuck yes." He grabs hold of my arm and lifts me from the floor before pushing me hard onto the bed.

His hands are all over me as he tears my panties clear off my body, leaving my thigh highs where they are. Armor pushes my legs all the way back until my knees are by my arms, and he dives face-first into my pussy.

"Oh shit!" I squeal and try to get away from the sudden onslaught of pleasure, but he doesn't let me go. I'm stuck, and I fucking love it.

He licks me from my entrance up to my clit and back again, making sure to pay the most attention where it matters.

My legs shake hard as a monstrous orgasm rips through my body.

"Give me all that shit. Fuck, I can't get enough," he says through gritted teeth as he licks up every drop of my arousal.

Finally, when my body is completely lax, he crawls up and notches the crown of his dick between my wet and sensitive folds.

"Tell me you know how much you mean to me," he orders, and I see in his eyes that he means it. It's crazy for me to think there's anyone else. My self-consciousness got out of hand, and he wanted me to know there was no reason for it. I asked him to prove it, and this is a good start.

"I know. I believe you, Armor. Only me. You only want me," I say, gasping for air both from the position and my need to have him inside of me.

"You better fucking believe it. I'm all yours, Jada," he says and thrusts hard.

He fills me swiftly, and I gasp loudly at the intense pressure.

"Oh god, oh god," I whimper over and over as he starts hammering into me.

"Say my fuckin' name," he orders.

"Armor, fuck me, yes!" I grab hold of his arms and just go along for the ride.

The man flips me in so many different positions I'm dizzy by the time he's ready to come. We end up in the doggy-style position, and every muscle in my body is trembling from overuse.

He grips my ass hard and roars out my name as he lets loose. I feel him coming deep inside of me, and for some reason, his cum is like a drug.

My mind goes blank, and the sweet feeling of exhaustion takes over.

He's winded, but he makes sure to bend down and kiss

my neck and back as he slides out of me. The bed is a mess, but I can't be bothered to move right now.

"I'd never hurt you like that," he tells me. I moan my acknowledgment, but in the back of my mind, it registers that he didn't say he'd never hurt me, period.

I just hope, whatever happens, the both of us are strong enough to get through it together.

CHAPTER FOURTEEN

Armor

She's pissed at me, and she has every right to be, but I know that last night wasn't enough to make it up to her. The fact of the matter is I feel like I'm being pulled in two different directions. One is my commitment to Jada in whatever it is we're doing together. Whereas the other is my efforts to be putting an end to the trafficking ring that's been plaguing Los Angeles. Last night, two parts of my life crossed, and I hurt the woman I cared about because of it. Now, I might've saved my ass by calling Inc. He corroborated everything I told Jada about the trafficking situation, and I know if he didn't answer and told her everything, the two of us wouldn't be together right now.

I keep thinking about what happened last night before I met up with Jada. José and Vik took me back to one of Vik's facilities. I was astonished a few times, but the fact they didn't even have me blindfold myself is shocking. You'd think they'd want to keep their location a secret from clients or any other people. Yet, they didn't bother to put up one safeguard with me.

I sat in the back of their SUV and watched as we left the industrial park, went a few miles down the road, and then drove into a part of Los Angeles I'd never gone to before. We rolled straight up to what looked to be like any other office building and then got out of the vehicle. Only, once we entered the office building, did I get the feeling this was covering up a lot more than just the trafficking Vik was doing.

As I blink, my memories pull me back to the previous evening.

"Come with me," Vik's words pull me out of my thoughts, and I follow him as he walks us past the security guard posted in the front of the building. This place looks like any other. There's a large reception area, with boards behind reception stating which units are rented by which businesses. Though, as I tear my eyes away from the board, I realize I saw the name 'The Orchid Corporation' on more than half of the building.

Vik and José walk toward the elevators, and I follow them into it as the doors open. Vik waits for the doors to close and then presses the button for the basement, but a red light comes on. "It's restricted access," he tells me.

The next thing I know, Vik puts his hands on a certification plaque in the elevator and pushes it upward. Behind the plaque, there's some sort of metal device, and it comes out about two inches, then a red light begins scanning. Vik stands in front of the red light, and after it scans up and down a couple of times, the red light turns off, the scanner goes back, and he puts the plaque back where it was a few minutes ago. "Retina scanners. You can never be too careful."

I don't bother responding because I have no reason to. He's careful here but yet didn't blindfold me or anything when they drove me out this way. Maybe Vik feels like he doesn't have to worry about anything because this location's security is at the top of the food chain.

The elevator begins taking us down, and before I know it, the doors are open, and the three of us are walking into more of an office than a basement. Sure, the walls are made of concrete . . . but Vik has a reception area with a waiting area, and there's a woman who's sitting behind the receptionist's desk. "Vik, it's lovely to see you. Are you looking for anything specific tonight?"

"Karina, yes. I want one of our longest residents to meet us in the conference room. I have a prospective new client here, and I want him to see what makes our girls different than the rest," *Vik smirks, and Karina nods, then goes on her way.*

José and I follow Vik to the conference room. The room is pretty much all concrete, from the walls to the floor to the table. It's all there is. The only things that aren't concrete are the one glass wall where we can see the hallway next to us, the chairs at the table, and the lighting.

"What type of girls and women do you or your clients look for? What sells the most for you?" *Vik asks.*

"I'm not sure what Otis has said about what I've purchased, but I've found that—"

"Otis has said nothing, as it's not his job to tell me what you want to buy. Is Otis on your payroll? Should he be telling me these things?"

Vik leans back in his chair and assesses my reactions to his words. "No, Otis isn't on my payroll, and I'm certain you know of that already. I only assumed, as a courtesy, Otis might tell you what I've purchased, so you could understand the types of things I'm looking for instead of wasting my time and asking me these questions now when I already have a very busy night. You've made me late for another meeting, so I'd prefer we get on with whatever spectacle you're planning."

"Ah, you're a man who honors his time. Still, I need answers to my questions," *Vik goes on, and José keeps directing his eyes between the two of us.*

"The Eastern European girls are the most sought after, but

Chinese are good too. Latinas tend to do well. The bottom line is, I'm always willing to try new things, as are my clients," I inform him and then look over to José.

The next thing I know, I spot Karina walking up the hallway with a teenage girl in a red dress. The girl's hair is practically as white as snow, and her features make me believe she's Eastern European, but she could be Swedish for all I know.

Karina comes up to the conference room doors, and Vik gives her a nod, then she enters with the girl. "Helena, please, come meet my friends." As Vik speaks, the girl walks over to him and stands beside him, then looks at José and then me. She smiles sweetly and looks between the two of us as she awaits some sort of instruction.

"Helena here has been with my organization for almost ten years. She'll be turning sixteen around Christmas, and as you can see, she is perfectly behaved. She will do whatever I command of her, as will the others. They don't fight back because they know what happens to them." Vik looks over at Helena, and she swallows hard.

"If we disobey, we'll have a higher price to pay." It's as if this saying is something that's been instilled in her head since she first arrived here. And it's exactly the sort of thing I'm looking to abolish. My club runs the streets here in Los Angeles, and once I have enough information on who the head honchos are, I can bring this to Breaker. I know he'll be pissed I haven't been entirely honest with him about what I've been doing, but this is all for the greater good.

I shake my head as the rest of the events from last night go through my mind. I have to stop this. I know I'm getting closer to the center of the trafficking rings here in Los Angeles, but it isn't happening fast enough.

My phone vibrates on my bedside table, pulling me from my inner turmoil. I need to get downstairs and see Jada. At least she distracts me from all of this, which is what I desperately need right now.

CHAPTER FIFTEEN

JADA

I can't stop the tears of joy running down my face as Fury tells Shiloh and me about the one time he was cornered in a room with a woman he didn't want to have sex with. Sometimes it's like a motion picture film, the shit these guys get themselves into.

"I'm serious. I was hopping over the bed and tables like I was jumping hurdles in an Olympic event, just up and over." Shiloh bangs her hand on the table, wheezes out for him to stop, and then looks at Hammer.

I take another glance at the two of them while they both continue to laugh, and I can feel the love radiating off them and myself. I feel like I'm home. I feel like I've earned my place here. Not just as Hammer's sister or Armor's woman, but just as Jada.

When I made the decision to stay here in Los Angeles, I did so because I needed a fresh start. Of course, Armor was an added bonus. Now I feel like I have everything I could have wanted in a new beginning.

Falling for Armor was an unexpected surprise, but one I'm so happy I got.

I love him. As scary as that might be, I realize that this thing between us is that forever type of love, and I'm not going to fight against it.

Just as Fury is about to say something else, a low, painful groan comes from the back, and we all turn our attention that way.

Sunny and Ice are rushing out. Ice grabs hold of Sunny's belly and stops walking. She moans and sways slowly from side to side, taking deep breaths. Ice is bogged down with a bag, his jeans, and his shoes, which he's trying to shove his feet into while still holding on to Sunny.

"Oh my god, what's happening?" I ask, getting up from my seat and going over to help so that he can get dressed.

"What's happening is that this baby is trying to make an entrance. This time it's not Braxton Hicks, that's for fucking sure," Sunny snaps out impatiently.

"Oh fuck," Fury says and takes one step back as if he doesn't know what he's supposed to be doing in the situation. Shiloh is quick to step forward, offering to help.

"What do you need? Do you want some ice? Are you going to make it to the hospital? Not Braxton Hicks this time?" Shiloh asks a flurry of questions, even though Sunny just said it wasn't Braxton Hicks.

"No way in hell is this Braxton Hicks. No way," Sunny moans again, and Ice hops up from the floor, one boot on, the other discarded.

"Get dressed. We got her." I push him away, and he looks at her worried before he drops back down to shove his feet into his shoes.

When I look up again, I don't see Fury anywhere. The wimp.

"I swear to God if you don't move your ass," Sunny yells,

and Ice moves even faster, taking his woman's harsh words to heart.

I smirk at him, knowing that this is all pregnancy pain. He's got a lot more of her screaming at him to put up with before that baby is here with us.

"Okay. I'm ready . . . we can go," he says and comes back to hold on to his woman.

"You guys going to be okay? You need someone to drive you?" I ask as Sunny starts walking again.

"No, we got it," he says, barely able to keep up with his woman, who is beelining straight for the door. She's on a mission, and that mission is to get that baby out of her.

I laugh, and Shiloh bites at her thumbnail. "Oh, I hope everything is going to be okay," she says aloud, and I pull her into a hug.

In her condition, I'm sure she's thinking about when this will be happening to her in a few months.

Once Sunny and Ice are out, Shiloh and I sit back down and have a little more girl talk before I see Armor rushing down the stairs to get to me.

"Hey, are you okay? Fury told us about the baby coming. Everything okay?" he asks.

I tilt my head to the side, not sure why he's so worked up right now, "Yeah, we're fine. We're not the ones pushing a watermelon out of our vaginas." I giggle while both he and Shiloh let out a pained whimper.

Armor rubs the back of his neck and takes a step back. "Damn, my bad. I just didn't want you to be upset or anything and not be here for you."

This man is as attentive as any person in the world. I'm lucky to have him.

"No need to apologize. I appreciate the concern, Armor." I wrap my arms around his neck and pull him in for a kiss. It still thrills me that I can do this in public without having to worry about anyone getting in trouble.

"Any plans for today?" he asks, wrapping his arms around my waist and pulling me closer.

"No, absolutely nothing."

"You want to go get something to eat with me?"

"Ooh, yes, please. I'll take all the alone time you want to give me." I scratch my fingers through the little hairs at the nape of his neck.

"If that's the case, then I have just the perfect place for us to go." He smiles.

I lean in closer and he kisses my forehead before he shoos me upstairs to get dressed. I don't know what he has planned, but whatever it is, as long as he's with me, I know it's going to be the best date possible.

* * *

A few hours later, we're eating tasty Thai food on the back deck of his beach house out in Malibu. He's picked me up some flowers and a decadent cake from a little bakery in town. We've got the deck all set up like a picnic, and he's turned the lights out, so the only light we're getting is from the moon. It's absolutely breathtaking and amazing that he would have thought to put something like this together on such short notice.

"Armor, every day you surprise me more and more," I whisper as I lean back against his chest with his arms around me, taking in the beautiful scenery in front of us.

"Well, I hope I keep surprising you. You'll let me know if I start slacking off," he jokes, and I shake my head.

"Not possible. I don't think you know how to take a day off. You're like the energizer bunny. You just keep going and going . . ." My words trail off, and I think about how that analogy can be applied to another part of our relationship.

The sex is so damn amazing.

"Yes, I can. In both ways, you're thinking." I turn around to see him waggling his eyebrows like an idiot and laugh.

"Not allowed to read my mind. That's not fair."

"Aww, but I like what's in there," he keeps up the joke.

It hits me that I have to tell him something else that's on my mind. I need to get it off my chest, only because I feel like I'm going to burst if I don't tell him soon. It may be quick, and part of me is nervous that he's going to think we're moving too fast, but I don't think it's the case. He shows me how he feels for me every day. His actions already speak much louder than any words could. I just want to get them out into the world.

"Well, can you see everything in there? Can you see that I'm hopelessly in love with you?" I ask, turning around in his arms, and he stops joking immediately.

"What?" he asks.

I kneel and repeat myself, staring into his eyes so he knows I'm telling the truth.

"Armor. I didn't expect any of this to happen with you, especially not this quickly, but I can't deny it. I love you."

He squeezes my thigh and puts a hand up to my chin, "I'm in love with you too, Jada. Every single part of you. Body and soul."

I lean forward to kiss him, suddenly so overwhelmed with joy from hearing him echo the exact words that just came out of my mouth. I was nervous about telling him, but now I couldn't be happier.

Happier or hotter for him.

I kiss him deeply, crawling through the space between us and straddling his lap. I'm happy I chose to wear a sundress because I don't want to worry about getting through my clothes.

"Take me, Armor. Right now," I whisper against his lips, and he lets out a soft grunt. His hands slide up my thighs, and he moves my panties to the side. I throw my head back and let the moonlight wash over my skin as he slips one finger inside of me, working me perfectly like only he knows how.

I lean forward again and make quick work undoing his pants and lifting only enough to push them down.

Suddenly, the air around us is sparking with sexual need. The slow, sensual movements from before are replaced with a desperate pulling off of clothes.

He yanks my dress over my head and lets my wild curly hair out of my hair tie. I'm already so wet for him that when he lines himself up with my slick folds, I simply lower myself down, and he slides right in.

"Ahh, fuck," he grits out, holding me close.

We stay there on the deck under the moonlight, wringing every last bit of pleasure from each other.

Somehow this feels different. It feels like a new level of pleasure because of our admission of love.

I came here to see what life had in store for me and got the best surprise anyone could ever offer me.

Armor.

CHAPTER SIXTEEN

Armor

Holy fuck, today there's been a serious change of events. It feels like yesterday we all found out Sunny and Ice were having a baby, and now they've been at the hospital for over a day. According to Jada, she's been in labor for over twenty-four hours . . . and I don't know how women do it. How the fuck do they endure that sort of pain for over a day? You think the doctor would've taken the baby by now, but they haven't.

Archer woke up sick, so I've been manning the bar. Just because I have an officer position within the club doesn't mean I won't help whenever we need it. Jada's been doing some content creation work on her laptop in our bedroom, but she said when she got finished with her work, she'd come down and help. She's been up there for about six hours, so hopefully, she'll come down soon. The dinner rush is going to be coming in at any minute, and while there are other brothers here, none of them enjoy being the barback.

"Hey there, sweetie pie!" a busty blonde woman says to

me as she sits down directly in front of me. I'm keeping to myself, wiping the inside of a glass, so it dries fully.

"What're you drinkin'?" I question the woman, and she smiles from ear to ear.

"What? Aren't you gonna ask for my ID?" she twirls a finger in her hair and looks me up and down. I know exactly what she's doing too. I've seen women like her do it a million and ten times. Not only is she ogling me like I'm a piece of meat, but she's acting like she could be under twenty-one, which we both know is crap. She has to at least be in her forties. The crow's feet around her eyes and wrinkles on her forehead are everything I need to know about her living an intense life.

Still, I put on my charm in the hopes she leaves a decent tip for the club. We split the tips here to put extra cash in each of our pockets. "Darlin', you're beatin' me to the punch here. I was just about to ask you for that."

"Well, here it is, and I'll have a Mai Tai." She hands me her ID, and I look at the birth year, confirming she is well in her forties.

"All right, I'll get that whipped up for you," I tell her as I go along the bar and get all of the ingredients for her drink. By the time I'm mixing it up, I spot Jada coming in from the back. Her hair's pulled up in a tight bun on the top of her head, and she's wearing a red top with dark jeans. She looks fucking beautiful, and I count myself as the luckiest man alive right now.

Jada comes up to the bar and sits a couple of barstools down from the woman I'm waiting on. I set her drink in front of her and tell her to let me know if she needs anything else. Meanwhile, Jada's leaning across the bar, and I walk over to give her a smooch. The woman I was just waiting on a moment ago scoffs, and Jada looks over at her. "Do you have a problem or something?"

"Yeah, I'm just so sick of the guys who look like him always being taken. There aren't any decent guys around anymore, that's for sure."

Jada presses her lips together in a frown. "I'm sure there's someone out there for you. You just have to be open to looking for him. I'm Jada, by the way." Jada scoots off the barstool and then goes over to where the woman is and shakes her hand.

"I'm Karmen. I just moved here from the midwest. Divorcee, my oldest kid, is nineteen and in college, but of course, no one cares about that. I came here for a new life, and I'm looking for a new man to be with it."

"I don't blame you. I just moved here from Montana," Jada tells her, and Karmen smiles lightly.

"I'm from Idaho. It's nice to meet you, Jada. Can I get your number, and maybe we can hang out sometime?" Karmen asks, and Jada nods.

For a while, Jada chats with Karmen, and I'm busy with the dinner rush as they begin to pour in. After about an hour, Karmen leaves, and Jada tells me she has plans to go out to dinner with her next week. I think it's really nice she offered to even give her number out and go out with Karmen in the first place.

"You know anyone single in the club who might be interested in her?" Jada asks me, and I think about it for a few seconds.

"Killer is the only one I can think about off the top of my head. He's around her age. I could maybe bring something up after you get to know her better." I'm not going to do it now. It won't be helpful, especially since we don't know if this woman is crazy or anything yet. But I'll let Jada get a feel for her first.

"Cool. So, did you hear the good news?"

I narrow my brows at her. "No, what news?"

"Sunny had the baby. It's a boy. They named him Hayden," Jada tells me, and I'm happy for both of them. Hayden will be the third son that Ice has ever had. He has Breaker, but I think he has another son too . . . but for all I know, that son could be Sunny's kid. I have a hard time keeping track of all the people Ice has had kids with. Fuck, me saying that is horrible. Most of his children are dead. Jesus, I'm a fucking asshole.

My phone buzzes in my back pocket, and I see it's Otis. I click on the message and read it.

From: Otis

Yo man. Got the address for another associate you might want to meet.

I immediately text him back.

To: Otis

Cool. Send it over. They wanna meet up tonight or what?

From: Otis

Yeah. He's down to meet you tonight.

To: Otis

Sounds good. What time?

From: Otis

8 p.m. on the dot. He's a stickler about being on time.

To: Otis

Got it. I'll be there.

Jada looks down at my phone and gives me a warning glance. I know what she's thinking, that it's risky, but I have to keep going down this path. "I'll be careful, just like I always am." She still doesn't stop staring at me the way she is, but I know if our roles were reversed, I'd be concerned about her safety as well.

CHAPTER SEVENTEEN

JADA

Time seems to be moving at an unearthly crawl. When Armor told me that he was going out for a run, I figured it was only going to take a little while, but he's been gone for hours already. As much as I don't want to, I'm starting to get worried. I know this comes with the territory, but it's still hard to get used to.

I'm trying not to stress it too much, but he's probably out trying to clear his head, which is exactly what I should be doing right now.

I grab the remote off the side table and flip on the TV. I pass through the channels in a flash, nothing reaching out and grabbing my attention. I like the feeling of being in Armor's room while he's not here. His smell and presence keep me somewhat calm. The fact that everyone now knows that he and I are together has made everything so much easier for us.

I thought for sure that my brother was going to have a coronary, but I'm happy that he's finally coming around to the idea.

I'm sure he didn't want his sister with anyone in the club, but out of anyone, he should know that Armor was going to do right by me and protect me. Not only him but everyone else as well. Doubly now because I'm not only Hammer's sister, but I'm Armor's woman.

Additionally, I'm excited about the fact that there's no longer a need for us to hide anything from anyone. There's nothing wrong with having a quick fuck in the closet, but I don't want that to be the only time I can put my hands on my man just because we're worried about someone seeing us.

When I've flipped through the channels at least six times in the hope of passing the time, I finally give up my search for something to keep my mind occupied and reach for my clothing to get changed into. As soon as I get them on and put on my shoes, I make my way up to the rooftop of the building. Shiloh's the first person I notice up there, and she looks like she's just enjoying a little sun at the moment. Laid out and relaxing.

"Jada, hey, what are you doing up here? I thought you were in for a nap," she says and sits up in her chair. Despite the fact that she's still pretty small, I'm beginning to see a little bit of a baby bump on her. She still has to move pretty slowly to make sure she doesn't get dizzy. When she moves, I always make sure that I'm paying attention to her, just in case she falls over while I'm around. The last thing we need right now is for something to happen to her. My brother would lose his fucking mind.

"I thought I would give it a go, but my racing mind is saying otherwise." I chuckle, and she joins me.

"Yeah, it's so dead today. I usually like that, but now I'm bored," she sighs.

"Well, what about taking a walk with me over the bridge?" I ask, thinking maybe a little bit of physical exercise will be enough to get my mind off the fact that Armor isn't back yet.

Shiloh scrunches up her nose and frowns. "Ugh, that means sweating and achy feet. Um, how about some food? I could go for something to eat right now." As she speaks, her eyes glaze over a little, and I know she's already thinking about whatever it is she wants to eat.

Far be it from me to keep a pregnant woman from getting some grub.

"Sure, let's go do that." I nod and put my hand out for her. She gets up slowly and joins me. We take our time and make our way to the clubhouse restaurant. Some of the guys are already there and either eating or drinking when we walk in.

Shiloh beelines straight for one of the tables, and the waitress comes over to get our order.

I was right when I thought that Shiloh was already thinking about what she wanted to eat. Before the waitress could get our menus down in front of us, she was already putting in her order.

We end up ordering some hot wings, probably more than the both of us could eat, mozzarella sticks, and some loaded cheesy fries.

Just thinking about it reminds me that I may need to go take that walk by myself to work off some of these calories. In Shiloh's case, she may be eating for two, but I'm definitely not.

Suddenly, Shiloh says, "I swear I'm going to blow this place up if she shows up here without the fucking ranch dressing." And she glances at the waitress who's walking toward the back to place our order.

I laugh at the intensity of Shiloh's statement. She's serious about her food.

I can only imagine how hard it is to be pregnant.

"So, what's going on? You look like you're on the razor's edge right now," Shiloh says as she takes a sip of the water in front of her. I pick up the fork that's sitting right on the side of the table and start to play with it between my fingers. I just want to expend some of this tense energy that I have. Even though I'm enjoying my time with Shiloh in the back of my mind, I'm still busy worrying about Armor.

"Nothing's really the matter. I guess I'm just a bit concerned." I do my best to downplay how I'm feeling. I don't want to get Shiloh worked up.

"About what?" she asks.

"Armor, of course. He went on a run a few hours ago, and he's not back yet. I keep waiting for the day. I'm not going to freak out when I don't see him for a few hours, but so far, that hasn't happened for me."

Shiloh nods her head and takes another big sip of water. "I know how you feel, and I'm sorry to tell you it's not going to get much easier than it is right now. Armor can take care of himself, though, and if he is in any trouble, the guys will be right with him in a flash. Being linked with someone from this club means there's always a possibility that shit can go bad, but ninety-nine times out of a hundred, everything is fine. He's probably out trying to clear his head or something like that," she says, echoing what I was thinking earlier.

"Yeah, I know it, but still, I'm not used to all the violence. He may be able to handle himself. I just hate that he's ever in those situations, to begin with." I let out a heavy sigh and shake my head, trying to clear my thoughts. I came here to stop thinking about this shit. I need to be focused on something else.

"Enough about that. How about you? How are you feeling?"

"Ugh, I'm just tired, then I'm tired of feeling tired. It's a never-ending cycle of one thing being wrong and then another. Just annoying. Don't get me wrong, I'm super excited about having this baby, but she's wreaking havoc on my hormones and my body," Shiloh complains, and I suck in a short gasp.

"She?" I ask excitedly. So far, they didn't know the gender of the baby, but I know they went to the doctor recently. Maybe they were able to find out.

"Oh, yup. Whoops, I guess I forgot to tell you. Hammer and I found out a few days ago that we're having a little girl." Shiloh smiles brightly, and I reach over for her arm and give her a squeeze. I'm so excited. I'm going to have another niece.

"That is so wonderful. I'm so damn happy for you two," I offer and swallow down the lump of emotions in my throat.

"Yeah, it's cool. I'm actually catching myself planning out outfits and how I'm going to do her hair. It's so silly." Shiloh laughs for a second before her attention is completely diverted by the waitress bringing our food. I say a quick prayer that she didn't forget the ranch dressing, and when I see the milky white substance placed on the table, I let out a sigh of relief. The last thing I want right now is to play referee between a pregnant lady and a waitress.

We stop talking for a little while as Shiloh quickly dives into her food. Just like I suspected, we're unable to eat much more than half of everything.

I lean back in my chair and bring the conversation back to the new baby girl. "What did Hammer have to say when he found out he was having another little girl?" I ask, genuinely interested.

"Oh, he's happy about it, too. He lit up like a fucking Christmas tree." Shiloh makes fun. "I've actually been rolling the name Naomi around in my mind, but I have to find a way to discuss it with Hammer. I don't know how he's going to like it." She shrugs, and I scrunch up my face as I pop another fry in my mouth.

"Girl, please, there's no reason for you to be scared about

it. Hammer loves you and this baby. I'm sure he'll love whatever name you choose." I nod, and Shiloh looks down as if she's still unsure.

"I don't want to take any part of this away from him. I truly love that name."

"He's going to love it," I say, again, so matter of factly.

Just as we continue talking, the restaurant doors open up, and a man in dark jeans and a dark shirt walks in. His eyes are searching, and instantly I know the man isn't here for the food.

He goes straight to the bar where Agony is and introduces himself. Shiloh and I are close enough that I can hear what he's saying.

"Hey, I'm Otis. I need to speak to someone regarding one of your members," he says, getting straight to the point.

"Yeah?" Agony says, and I see Breaker come up beside him. "Which member would that be?"

"Armor. The dude is in way over his fuckin' head," Otis says, and the hair on the back of my neck stands up.

Is he in trouble? Is that why this man is here? I start to breathe fast, and Shiloh puts a hand on my arm to keep me seated.

"What the hell do you mean by that?" Agony asks.

"He's digging into some shit that's going to get him fucked up. I don't know what you got to do to get him to stand down, but you need to," Otis says.

I can't contain myself anymore. I turn in my chair and stare at the men behind the bar, which was the wrong thing to do. Breaker finally notices me there.

"Stop talking. Come with me," he says to the man, and instantly the only link I have to knowing what's going on is ushered behind closed doors.

"Everything is okay. This could be about something else from before. We don't know," Shiloh says, and I give her a wobbly smile. I feel like I'm going out of my mind with worry.

All of these questions are running around in my mind, and no one is answering them. I pull my phone out of my purse and look down to see if Armor has called, but there are no notifications. I say a silent prayer that he's alright and wait on pins and needles for someone to come out and say something to me.

A few minutes feel like an hour, but suddenly the doors to the back open up, and everyone walks back out. Breaker, Otis, and a few other patched members all walk with purpose out of the restaurant, leaving only Agony, Archer, and Fury in the bar.

No one tells me anything, and I look over to Agony for some inclination as to what's going on.

"Breathe, baby cakes. It's handled," he says and goes back to tending the bar.

I'm not sure whether that's supposed to soothe me or not, but it definitely doesn't. If something has to be handled, that means something is going on right now.

Armor may be in trouble. This could be the one in a hundred that Shiloh was talking about earlier.

I drop back against my seat and put a hand up to my face. I can't take this. I need to know that he's all right.

All I have now is a promise that his brothers are going to be there for him. I just hope it's enough.

CHAPTER EIGHTEEN

Armor

Chains comes in to relieve me from being the bartender for the night, and I promise Jada I'll be careful when I go out, but what I don't let Jada see is that I got a pretty intense text message from Otis after the ones she saw. Otis essentially accused me of hiding some shit from him, and he's right . . . but I'm not here to take him down. He's a sort of broker with everyone, but I know Otis has more than just his hands in this shit. He deals with drugs, prostitutes, and the like. Whatever he can do to make money, he's going to do.

I met up with Otis before I was supposed to go meet up with this new player he told me about. Otis had photos of me with my cut on from the Satan's Raiders MC, so I had no choice but to be honest with him. I thought he was going to throw me to the wolves, but he asked me about what I was trying to do. So, I told him what I was doing, getting kids out of these fuckers' hands. He told me he was looking for a way out of this business, but the man I'm supposed to meet up with tonight has something over his head. I don't know what it is, but I'm sure in time, I'm going to find out. I ended up making a deal with Otis. He keeps my cover, and I'll help him get out. We can kill two birds with one stone.

After I met up with Otis, he eventually texted over the address to the building where I was supposed to meet this guy at. When I read the address, it seemed really familiar. I couldn't place it at first, but now that I'm pulling into the parking garage of the building, an overwhelming sense of déjà vu comes over me.

This building is owned by my father. It's actually his LLC's corporate office. "Fuck," I mutter under my breath as I get out of the vehicle and head for the elevators. I take the elevator up to the lobby and then glance down at my text message. It says to go to the eighth floor, so I do that. Only, I know what the eighth floor of this building is. It's where the head honchos are, including my father's office. I'm instructed to wait in the seating area until someone comes to fetch me, so I sit back in a part of the waiting area that can't be seen by the offices and wait until someone comes up.

Only a few minutes later do I hear the tapping of feet against the wooden floors, and just as my greatest fear courses up my bones, I'm in complete shock. I'm staring at someone I very well knew could be the person I was meeting tonight once I pulled into the parking garage—my father.

"I didn't expect you to be here. I'm actually waiting for a business associate. Do you care if we meet up tomorrow at some point? Maybe over lunch or dinner?" Ah, he doesn't realize the person he's going to meet and I, are one and the same.

I let out a breath I didn't even know I was holding in and looked him right in the eyes. "I'm the person you're supposed to be meeting, Dad."

Just like that, the realization comes over him. He doesn't

know what to do at first, and I watch as he tries to figure out what to do next. He isn't sure what he should be doing. I'm sure he's wondering if he should be proud of me right now or cautious.

"I can't believe you're in this shit, honestly. I never thought you would be as callous and sickening to do this shit."

My father swallows and looks at me with stern eyes. "Maybe you should leave if you're not cut out for this business."

I rise from my seat and stare straight into his eyes. "I'm not going to leave. Not at all. This is bullshit, fuckin' bullshit. You make money off selling children, Dad. What sort of sick bastard does that? How could you, of all people, do it?"

My father shrugs his shoulders nonchalantly. "My father did it before me and his father before him. It's something we've passed down from generation to generation. It's how we've made a name for ourselves. How we all live comfortably." He can't be saying what I think he's saying. There's no way.

"You've never told me this before now. How do I know it isn't all bullshit?" He could be making this up right now, and I wouldn't put it past him. My father's always played dirty in business, and sure I knew that . . . but I didn't know he'd be like this.

"You never seemed right to bring into this. Why would I tell you unless I thought you could handle it?"

It was never about me 'handling' it, as he says. It was only about my complacency.

"The way you're looking at me right now tells me you can't handle it, and you came here for some other reason. What reason would that be, son? Hmm?" My father reaches around his back, pulls out a gun, and before I know it, he has fired, and I'm hitting the ground.

I pull my gun out and fire over and over again until he hits the ground. My vision becomes hazy, and the next thing I know, the darkness is taking over me. I don't know if I'm going to make it out alive this time.

CHAPTER NINETEEN

JADA

My eyelids flutter as I feel Armor's hands run down my body.

"God, that feels good."

"I know, babe. That's what I'm here for, to make you feel good." I reach out to him, but I can't reach wherever he is. When he slips a finger between the wet folds of my pussy, I let my hands fall back down to the bed. I can always count on him to take care of me, no matter what's going on. He's always making sure that I'm good. That's one of the things that I love about him so much. When it comes to pleasing me, he never takes any shortcuts to achieve that goal, even if that means he might have to wait for his pleasure to become a reality.

"I'm all yours, Jada," he says, and I groan, frustrated at the fact that I can't touch him. Just as I'm about to reach release, my eyes pop open, and I realize that instead of being in his room, I'm someplace else. Someplace very dark. I don't feel safe anymore. I want Armor. I need him closer.

"Armor, where are you?" I call out for him, but I still only feel his hands on my body. I can't touch him. I look up for him, but it

feels like the room just gets darker. My heart beats rapidly in my chest as the pleasure shifts into fear.

"Armor."

"I'm here, Jada. I will always be here for you," he says, but it seems his voice is so far away from where I am.

"Armor!" I call out for him louder and try to get up from the bed, but it feels like a weight is holding me down.

What the hell is this? What's going on? I try not to panic. Not with him here with me. Armor's going to protect me. Always.

"Armor, please. I'm scared," I whimper in the darkness and reach blindly for him again.

"I'm here. I'm always going to be here," he says, and then his hands are no longer on me.

"No, please. Come to me." I put my hand out, expecting him to take it, but I feel nothing but air.

"I'm here, Jada," he whispers again, and now I know for sure that he's moving away. I'm alone. He's going to leave me all alone here in this strange place. I can't take it.

"Armor!" I scream and scream for him.

Emotions clog up my throat, and I hiccup past the tears that begin to stream down my face. He can't leave me, not when I finally got him. Not when we're so damn good for each other.

"Armor!" I scream again long and hard.

I strain against whatever is holding me down until it feels like I can't breathe. I fall deeper into the darkness. Farther away, deeper and deeper until I can't feel anything. I can't hear him anymore. Armor's gone.

* * *

I jerk upright in the bed, a shuttered gasp leaving my mouth as I blink a few times and take in the surrounding environment. The lights are on, and my hands grip the same sheets that were on the bed the day before.

"It was a dream. Just a dream . . . just a dream." I say to myself over and over again, but it doesn't stop the tears that are streaming down my face. I've never really had such vivid dreams before, and if that's any example, I'd rather not have anymore.

I suck in a few deep breaths, trying to get myself back into a calm state.

I seem to always get so amped up whenever Armor's out on a run, and now with this one taking longer than usual, it seems like my fears are slipping over into my dreams.

I swing my unsteady legs over the side of the bed and force myself to move. I need to shake the last bits of this dream away. Armor's fine. I know he is.

I walk over to the bathroom and splash some water on my face. A deep pink blush is on my cheeks from the crying and excitement that I was just going through. I look like absolute hell. I spend a few minutes going over some breathing techniques, and when I leave the bathroom, I start to feel more like myself.

Even though it's bright in the room thanks to the lights, I glance at the clock and realize that it's pretty late. Maybe Armor called while I was sleeping.

I speed walk over to the table and pick up my phone, wishing with everything I am that there are a few missed calls or some texts to put my mind at ease. When I don't see anything from him, my heart drops a bit. I know while he's on a run, it may be impossible for him to call me. I just need to wait.

Just as I'm about to turn the TV on and find something to drown out my worries, I hear the door to the clubhouse open.

I expect there to be a bunch of footsteps, heavy and hard, but I only hear one set. Fast moving and coming in my direction. I hold the remote in my hand, my knuckles going white due to my grip. When the door to my room flies open, and I see Shiloh, I feel the tight grip of dread wrapping around my gut. I don't know why, but something tells me I need to stand up right now, so I do.

Something's wrong.

"Jada, you have to come now. Armor's been shot," she says, and I nearly fall down from the shock of it all.

"No, you're lying. No, no, no," I say as panic threatens to overtake every thought I have in my mind.

Shiloh rushes over to me and grabs my shoulders. "I know. But we don't have time. We need to go right now. I don't know how bad it is. The club's already at the hospital," she says, and hearing that everyone's already with Armor lets me know that this is very serious. I need to get to him. This time he's the one that needs protecting, and I'm not going to let him down.

* * *

Shiloh drives me to the hospital, and the entire ride there, I pepper her with questions that she doesn't know the answer to. She does her best to keep me calm, but the more she does, the more frantic I get. I want some answers. I want to hear Armor's voice one more time.

I don't even bother with the security guard who tries to stop me from running to the elevator. I don't have time for rules. Shiloh is right behind me, and I curse the seconds as they tick by.

Now that I know for certain that Armor's hurt, it feels like everything is moving so slowly.

I burst out of the elevator and sprint right toward the waiting room that Shiloh tells me the guys are in. She gets winded and falls behind but tells me to go on.

When I get in the room, it's only the guys from the clubhouse, no other patient families.

Everyone looks worried.

When they see me, it's like everyone's been rendered mute. No one utters a word.

A huge tear pops out of my eyes as I wait to hear the bad news.

"What's happened? Someone tell me, please," I cry, and Hammer is the one to come up to me. I grab hold of his shirt, balling my hands into fists against his chest. I need his strength right now.

"Hammer, what happened? How bad is it? Is he okay?" I ask and search my brother's eyes for some hope.

"I don't know. The doctors rushed him into surgery. I'm sorry." He wraps me in his arms, and I break down against his chest. I don't want to hear, 'I don't know'. I want to hear that he's fine. I want to hear Armor will be out in a minute. The last words I want to hear are, 'I don't know'.

I cry in my brother's arms for what feels like forever, just waiting for one of the medical staff to come in and tell me something. The silence is the most nerve-racking part of it all. At least if Breaker or Fury were cursing up a storm, I'd feel like this was a bit normal, but right now, all any of them are doing is sitting here in reverent silence.

Finally, after waiting for more than two hours, a doctor comes into the room. Everyone jumps up to get word on Armor's condition. I stand next to Hammer and hold on to him again for strength.

"I need to speak with the patient's family."

"We're all his family," Breaker says, and the doctor stutters, clearly overwhelmed by such a showing.

"Okay, well, we have good news." He gives a tentative smile, and I hear others heave out a sigh of relief. I wait for the doctor to continue before I do the same.

"The bullet did manage to pierce his pericardial sac, and there was a little damage to the muscle wall itself. Luckily, his heart is strong, and we were able to get to him in time. There's still some work to be done in the surgery, but so far, his prognosis is very good. As long as he takes it easy for a little while, I don't see any reason why he shouldn't make a full recovery." The smile on the doctor's face gets wider, and all the rest of the clubhouse go over to give their thanks.

I want to do the same, but it feels like my feet are stuck in the mud. I can't move.

"Is it okay?" I turn to my brother. I need to make sure that I'm not hearing things. I need to be sure that the doctor said that Armor's going to be okay.

Hammer puts both hands on my face and cradles my cheeks.

"Yes, Jada. He's going to be fine. I should've known that there was no way a little bullet to the chest was going to be enough to put that man down." He laughs, and I want to feel that same joy, but I can't break myself out of this terror.

"I want to see him," I say, and the doctor looks over everyone's shoulder to see me.

"He's still in surgery. They are closing him up now. Once we get him out to a recovery room, he can have visitors. Don't worry, miss, he's in good hands." The doctor nods his head once and turns on his heels to walk out the door.

None of this feels real, and I find myself wishing that I was still sleeping.

At some point, Hammer guides me back to one of the chairs, and he starts talking to me. Nothing of importance, probably just trying to get me to react.

"Come on, Jada. Please talk to me. You're scaring me," I hear Hammer say, and it's only then I can force my mouth to move.

My throat feels like sandpaper, and my body vibrates from all the anxiety surging through me.

"I'm okay, bro. Just shocked." I pat his hand, and he nods as if he understands.

"I know. What can I do? How can I help you?" he asks, and I try to swallow again, only to feel the pain in my throat.

"Can I have some water?" I ask, and Hammer rushes to get me what I ask for. He comes back with a small cup. My hands are shaking so much that I can't even take it from him. He ends up having to put it up to my mouth for me, so I can take a sip.

It feels good, and I drink a little more.

"There's my girl. Come on, take some more," he says, encouraging me.

I guess, in some sense, I'll always be Hammer's baby girl, but in my heart, I know the only person I want to hear say that is Armor.

Another hour later, a nurse comes out to let us know that Armor is out of surgery and in the recovery room.

"One person can go see him now," she says, and I'm surprised that Breaker tells me to go on.

I use Hammer's arm to get myself up to my feet and will myself to follow the nurse back to Armor's room.

"He's going to be a little groggy, so don't be alarmed if he falls asleep in the middle of a conversation," she tells me as she leaves me at his door.

I can't take another step. That mud that was keeping me locked in place has come back, and I'm stuck again.

The room looks so sterile. The white sheets, white bed, white walls. He's covered and tubes and wires that are hooked up to various machines. I'm not used to seeing him in such a vulnerable state. He looks so beat up part of me starts to believe that they were wrong about him being okay.

Only when he opens his eyes do I let out a strangled

breath. I rush over to the bed, pulling the chair closest to him with me, and grab for the hand that doesn't have the IV in it.

"Oh, Armor, what kind of mess did you get yourself into?" I fuss at him. Now that I know he's truly okay, I can't stop touching him. Making sure to move slowly, so I don't cause him any pain. "I was so fucking scared for you," I say, and he gives me a half-smirk.

"Don't be scared, babe. I already told you I'm all yours. Nothing's going to take me away from you."

He's said the words many times, but the weight of them now feels like a warm security blanket over my shoulders. I lean down and kiss his lips, making sure to stay away from the large bandage on his chest.

"You just had to go do it, didn't you?" I raise an eyebrow at him, poking fun at the situation.

"Of course. You know I couldn't let him get away with it."

I scoff and fall back into the chair, never letting go of his hand. "Yeah, 'cause you're stubborn as can be."

That gets a soft chuckle out of him, and finally, this nightmare of a day is turning into a dream.

EPILOGUE

JADA

Three Years Later...

I close my eyes as the brisk, salty breeze flows over my face.

There's no way that things could get any better than they are right now.

This is my dream come true.

My hands run down the white and pale red lace party dress that I've chosen to wear for the small celebration. I told Armor we didn't need it, but he refused to just let me give up on a dream I had.

"Wait, put that over there," I call out to one of the resort workers as they bring my lantern decorations out from the back. My toes dig into the sand as I rush over to help out. Of course, the resort promised that everything would be to my liking, but of course, I can't just give up control like that.

After all, how many times does a girl get their dream wedding?

After Armor was shot, I just couldn't stand to wait and have some big elaborate wedding, even though, in my heart, that's what I really wanted. He tried to make me see reason, but I told him that I wanted to marry him right away, and nothing he was going to say would make me change my mind.

In typical Armor fashion, he did what he had to do to make it happen. The minute he was able to stand upright, we went right to the courthouse, and he gave me his last name.

I was over the moon to be his wife, and ever since then, he made sure to do his best, not only to show me that I was a priority in his life but to make sure that I always felt safe and appreciated. For a big bad biker man, he sure does know how to make me melt in his hands.

Everything moved on in our lives quickly, according to him. One day about three months ago, we were watching TV, and I let it slip that I would've loved to have a beach wedding, that it would be my absolute dream.

That was all the reason Armor needed. He damn near demanded that I plan a full wedding like I wanted, and we would renew our vows the right way, with all of our family and friends present. The way we both deserved to have it done.

Once I got over the fact that he wasn't going to let this go, I got right to work planning my dream wedding here in Fiji. Not only is the island absolutely breathtaking, but it has been the only place I could ever see my wedding taking place.

At first, I was worried about the cost and then about what it would be like to get all of our family to travel this far, but Armor made sure I had nothing to worry about. Anytime there was a doubt in my mind, he was right there to erase it. At one point in our lives, he told me that he was a lucky man to have someone like me, but in reality, I'm more than lucky to have someone like him. I'm blessed.

I only hope that I can make him as happy as he makes me.

Even with all the drama of the clubhouse and the bad shit

that tends to happen to us, I can't imagine having my life without him and all his drama. Now, for the second time, I'm going to be able to declare that to the world when I walk down the aisle tomorrow and into Armor's arms.

"How's this? Better?" The resort worker asks, not upset at all that I basically ran onto the venue site and told him how to do his job.

"Yes. Much. Thank you." I smile at him and make a note to find a way to give all these people a very hefty tip. Though I'm sure Armor's going to take care of that too.

"Running away from me already?"

I turn my head at the sound of Armor's voice and can't stop the large smile that breaks across my face. He's always making me happy.

"Never. I'm all yours, Armor," I say as I walk over to where he is.

He's got on a pair of dark linen pants and a t-shirt that accentuates not only his muscles but the tats that snake up and down his arms. His facial hair is trimmed neatly, and if I didn't know any better, I'd say he was a clean-cut gentleman. Only I know the truth. There's nothing clean about my man. He's as dirty as they come, and I love it.

He grabs hold of me around my waist and pulls me closer to him, letting me feel his growing erection. "You better stop looking at me like that, or I'm going to have to call this party off."

I throw my head back and laugh before I wind my arms around his neck, loving the way his hands feel on my body even through the thin fabric of my dress.

"So many people, we can't do that," I say and lean up to place feather-soft kisses on his lips and cheek.

"The fuck we can't." He grinds into me harder, and a low moan falls from my mouth. He kisses me hard, and I feel the passion already starting to ramp up between us. You'd think, after all these years together, we'd be able to control ourselves in public.

Nope.

"No. Absolutely not! You two, stop it!" Shiloh calls out, causing Armor and I to pull away from each other.

"Could you be any more annoying?" I ask her, leaning against my man's chest.

"Yes, I can. Could you two be any more gag-worthy? You got all week to have all the sex you want. Tonight, we party!" she says and grabs my hand, pulling me away from Armor.

This is the one time she's let loose since she had Naomi, and I hate to think that I'm going to be a downer at the party simply because I want to feel Armor deep inside of me. She's right. We've got a whole week to lay in bed and do nothing but fuck. Besides, this may be the last time I get to party for a long time.

I turn my head briefly and see Armor walking slowly behind us. His pants were still tented slightly from his erection. I laugh more, and he just shakes his head.

Shiloh is the cock block of the year.

She pulls me into the main ballroom, where all the clubhouse and our family are busy guzzling liquor and dancing. When they see me walk back in, I'm pulled onto the dance floor, and instantly I'm not thinking about anything else but having the time of my life.

Even Breaker comes out a few times to dance with me, which tickles me to no end.

The guys wind up having shit tons to drink, and even before the party is halfway over, I'm starting to worry that half of them may not wake up for the ceremony tomorrow.

Not too worried, though. I know Armor would drag each one of them out of their room if he knew it would make my day better.

With all the activity and being on a tropical island, the

heat starts to get to me, and I have to pull my hair up and fan my face. Armor sees me and comes over with a drink in his hand.

"Here, babe, you're going to get dehydrated. I haven't seen you drink anything all day." He pushes the cold cocktail into my hand, and I stare down at it, knowing that this is where the secrets end. How the hell he thinks alcohol is going to hydrate me is laughable.

"No, I'm okay." I try to give the drink back, and he just shoves it back in my direction.

"You're hot and sweating. Since when do you not like these?" he asks, squinting his eyes at me.

Once Armor knows something's wrong, he's not going to let go.

"I like them. I just . . ." I trail off.

I was going to tell him tomorrow after the wedding, but I guess there's no time like the present.

"You just what? What's the matter? I promise I won't let you get drunk if that's what you're worried about," he says, while he puts my drink down on the table and waits for me to answer him.

"No, I just can't drink that." I smile at him, and he shakes his head, still not understanding why.

I lean up, so I can speak directly into his ear. "Doctor's orders," I scratch the back of his neck tenderly, "And I'm sure you agree, Daddy."

He pulls back sharply and looks me in my eyes before his eyes fall to my stomach. It's still flat, so I know he can't see anything. I rub in a small circle anyway, just to further drive my point home. His eyes jump back up to mine. He opens his mouth to speak, but nothing comes out. He licks his lips and starts again.

"You're pregnant?"

I nod.

"Really? You're fucking pregnant?" he says louder and turns.

"What! You're pregnant?" Shiloh squeals loudly, causing everyone to stop what they're doing and look at me. I nod again.

"I'm pregnant," I say loud and proud.

Armor's face lights up, and he nearly tackles me in a hug. Lifting me off the ground while a round of whoops and happy screams erupt around us.

"Oh, Jada, thank you. I love you so fucking much. I'm all yours, for fucking ever," he says as he puts me down. Smiling and kissing me tenderly.

"And I'm yours, Armor."

AUTHOR'S NOTE

I hope you all enjoyed Armor and Jada's story! Next up is Fury's Torment which releases next month. I'm really excited to let you guys know that starting with Fury's book I'm going to be having a co-writer join me in finishing out the rest of the series.

In June of this year I was in a really bad car accident and to sum things up, I hit my head really, really hard. It becomes a lot for me to stare at the computer for multiple hours a day, so I'm adding co-writers to quite a few of my series to help me finish them out faster for you guys. I don't want any of you to have to wait years for me to be back at one-hundred percent again.

The co-writer I'm adding to the Satan's Raiders MC is Lena Bourne, and she's an absolute delight. I can't wait for you guys to see what we're creating together with Fury's book!

ABOUT THE AUTHOR

Elizabeth is a romantic suspense author most popular for her motorcycle club and mafia books. While Elizabeth loves to write she is an avid reader as well who reads a mixture of genres. She lives in the North-Eastern United States on a farm with her rescue animals. When she isn't working you can find her spending time with her family, camping, or binge watching the latest trending show on Netflix.

ALSO BY ELIZABETH KNOX

Elizabeth Knox

Skulls Renegade MC

Reapers Rejects MC

Reapers Rejects MC: Second Generation

Satan's Raiders MC

Iron Vex MC: New York City

Knights of Retribution MC

Sons of Gods MC

Steele Bros

Love Hack

Mackenzies

Raiders of Valhalla MC

Deathstalkers MC

Stonewall Dynasty

The Mafia Brotherhood

Elizabeth Knox & Elle Knox

One Standalones

Elizabeth Knox & Raven Scott

Mafia Heirs: The Gallaghers

-

Elizabeth Knox & Emily Sharp

(Co-writer has changed to Rae B. Lake as of Summer 2022)

O'Dea Crime Family

<u>Elizabeth Knox & Iris Sweetwater</u>

The Clans